THE CRITICS DEBATE

General Editor: Michael Scott

The Critics Debate

General Editor Michael Scott

FURTHER TITLES ARE IN PREPARATION

THE GREAT GATSBY

Stephen Matterson

MACMILLAN

First published 1990 by
MACMILLAN EDUCATION LTD
Houndmills, Basingstoke, Hampshire RG21 2XS
and London
Companies and representatives
throughout the world

ISBN 0–333–48306–5 hardcover
ISBN 0–333–48307–3 paperback

A catalogue record for this book is available
from the British Library.

Printed in Hong Kong

Reprinted 1991

For Jean, who gave so much

Contents

General Editor's Preface

OVER THE last few years the practice of literary criticism has become hotly debated. Methods developed earlier in the century and before have been attacked and the word 'crisis' has been drawn upon to describe the present condition of English Studies. That such a debate is taking place is a sign of the subject discipline's health. Some would hold that the situation necessitates a radical alternative approach which naturally implies a 'crisis situation'. Others would respond that to employ such terms is to precipitate or construct a false position. The debate continues but it is not the first. 'New Criticism' acquired its title because it attempted something fresh calling into question certain practices of the past. Yet the practices it attacked were not entirely lost or negated by the new critics. One factor becomes clear: English Studies is a pluralistic discipline.

What are students coming to advanced work in English for the first time to make of all this debate and controversy? They are in danger of being overwhelmed by the cross currents of critical approaches as they take up their study of literature. The purpose of this series is to help delineate various critical approaches to specific literary texts. Its authors are from a variety of critical schools and have approached their task in a flexible manner. Their aim is to help the reader come to terms with the variety of criticism and to introduce him or her to further reading on the subject and to a fuller evaluation of a particular text by illustrating the way it has been approached in a number of contexts. In the first part of the book a critical survey is given of some of the major ways the text has been appraised. This is done sometimes in a thematic manner, sometimes according to various 'schools' or 'approaches'. In the second part the authors provide their own appraisals of the text from their stated critical standpoint, allowing the reader the knowledge of their own particular approaches from which their views may in turn be evaluated. The series therein hopes to introduce and to elucidate criticism of authors and texts being studied and to encourage participation as the critics debate.

Michael Scott

Introduction

In the Preface to his 1977 book on F. Scott Fitzgerald, the revision of a work first published in 1963, the critic Kenneth Eble took the opportunity to consider the strength of Fitzgerald's popularity and reputation during the preceding years. He noted various film and television productions based on Fitzgerald's novels, as well as the large number of critical books, scholarly articles, memoirs, and dissertations which had also appeared. Such a large amount of secondary work testified, Eble argued, to Fitzgerald's 'durability' as a writer. However, he went on, the cycle of Fitzgerald's popularity might well be coming to an end. He cited two major reasons for this: Americans might become less preoccupied than before with success, and fiction writers assuming popularity in the late 1970s were departing from the realist tradition in which Fitzgerald's novels are rooted. Accordingly, decreasing preoccupation with success would make Fitzgerald's interest in the subject less relevant to a future generation. Along with the technical advances in literary ideas and concepts, Eble implied, the novels of Fitzgerald would seem anachronistic and unsophisticated.

However, since Eble wrote his Preface, there seems to have been no abatement of interest in Fitzgerald. A film of *The Last Tycoon* has been produced in Hollywood, with a screenplay by Harold Pinter. A BBC production of *Tender is the Night* was adapted by another leading British writer, Dennis Potter. There has been no lessening of critical and scholarly interest in Fitzgerald; and, strikingly, all of his novels are widely available in Penguin editions. The *Collected Short Stories* was published by Penguin in 1986, and Zelda Fitzgerald's novel *Save Me the Waltz*, has been made available, along with Andrew Turnbull's selection of Fitzgerald's letters. All of these facts testify, in spite of Eble's predictions, to that same 'durability' of Fitzgerald's work.

The Great Gatsby has a life in different contexts, and to a large degree, the kind of novel that people discuss — that 'critics debate' — depends upon the perspectives from which they have chosen to view it. To the reader interested in Fitzgerald's life, there is ample material for a purely biographical approach. The novel is widely taught on courses in American Studies, with the assumption that it reveals something of the character of the American nation or culture at a given historical moment. A different approach might be to look at Fitzgerald's use of the Romantic tradition in literature, and at how his most famous novel relates to that tradition. Or, is it a novel best approached in terms of literary modernism — as a specific product of the mid-1920s? To some degree all of these approaches are valid, and all have been used by critics. In the contemporary critical climate, there are further issues that might usefully be raised in relation to this novel. Is Fitzgerald's treatment of women in the novel a major weakness? In what ways does it survive as a novel — how does it speak to us over sixty years after it was written, and what does it have to say? These are the kinds of questions that have assumed a critical validity during the past twenty years. It is also true that some of the developments in the novel genre, cited by Eble, have made possible other approaches to *The Great Gatsby*. In a counter-realist climate, the self-conscious narrator is a common figure; is it possible for us now to see Nick Carraway as such a narrator? For many readers and critics he has been an untrustworthy figure; thanks to the development of counter-realism, further emphasis could be placed on this aspect, with a fresh series of ideas about the novel. In short, the critical perspectives that can be adopted towards this novel are never necessarily fixed; they are always open to change, and it is a testimony to that continuing durability of Fitzgerald's work that we are still debating many of them.

For Part One of this book I have distinguished some of the most common approaches to the novel, and they are discussed in turn. Briefly, these are the mythic interpretations, the formalist emphasis, the place of *The Great Gatsby* in Fitzgerald's other writings, the socio-historical approach, and the questions raised about the novel's characters. While it is helpful to separate these approaches, it is important also to recognize that they do not necessarily exist separately from each other. For example, a particular approach to the character of Carraway influences other judgements about the novel. If one critic decides that he is an untrustworthy narrator, there will be inevitable implications for that critic's understanding of the novel's themes. Some of the possible approaches result in similar conclusions about the novel, while conflict and debate also arise. In Part Two of the book I examine some these issues in more detail, choosing several of the novel's themes that seem worthy of attention by a contemporary reader.

Throughout the book I have referred to the Penguin edition of *The Great Gatsby*. While the novel has been much reprinted in Penguin, the pagination has remained constant. The reader will note, however, that in referring to the character Meyer Wolfsheim, I have departed from the Penguin edition's spelling of his name as 'Wolfshiem'. This has been a standard practice among critics, referring back to the spelling in the novel's American editions.

Part One
Survey

The Great Gatsby and Myth

While *The Great Gatsby* is a novel much debated by critics and readers, there has been a general consensus that in a variety of ways the novel attains the status of a myth, and that Gatsby is a sort of mythical hero. The debate that has developed is over the kind of myth that *The Great Gatsby* is. Briefly, the critical issue is whether or not Fitzgerald was writing a myth specifically about America and American society, or whether the themes of *The Great Gatsby* transcend such particulars of time and place, and attain a wider relevance.

Before I start to examine these issues, though, the reader should be aware that in the 1920s many modernist writers saw the literary possibilities offered by myth. The most prominent of these writers were T.S. Eliot and James Joyce. In *The Waste Land* (1922) Eliot had evoked a sense of the sterility and meaninglessness of modern existence, partly by a series of complex contrasts with a past of mythic possibility. In the same year, Joyce's *Ulysses* had made the wanderings of one man through Dublin reflect the mythic episodes of Homer's *Odyssey*. Both writers had seen how the meanings of myths were relevant to a modern search for meaning in life. F. Scott Fitzgerald began writing *The Great Gatsby* in 1922, the year that saw the publication of *The Waste Land* and *Ulysses*, and was a fervent admirer of Eliot's poem (there are echoes of it in *The Great Gatsby*). But the kind of myth embodied in Fitzgerald's novel is quite different, in part since he does not rely on external established myths in order to explore his theme.

The American myth

One of the commonest critical approaches to *The Great Gatsby* has been to see it as a new myth of America, a myth partaking of the flavour of the 1920s, though this view has not been without dissenters. In 1954 the critic John Bicknell began an essay on *The Great Gatsby* by confidently asserting that at last readers were beginning to approach Fitzgerald not merely as a novelist of the Jazz Age, but as someone whose writing transcended the narrow concerns of one particular place or time (Bicknell, 1954, p. 556). Even now, this seems rather a premature judgement, in that many readers still regard Fitzgerald as a writer firmly rooted in the 1920s, but the point made is an important one. One of the qualities of myth is that it should be timeless, pointing to the universal, and thus not limited by the specifics of time and place. A recent essay by a leading Fitzgerald scholar, Matthew Bruccoli, has demonstrated the strategies used by Fitzgerald to make the novel transcend time and place. He refrained from over-use of the popular songs of the day; he did not identify current celebrities (as he easily could have done); and he deliberately used a strategy of vagueness. For example, the make of the car which kills Myrtle Wilson, 'the most famous car in American literature', is never identified (Bruccoli, 1985, pp. 6–7).

Powerful though these arguments are, the weight of critical opinion is in favour of viewing *The Great Gatsby* as a novel about the 1920s. If this is a mythic novel, it is inextricably involved with one particular time and place: furthermore, it is an examination of American myths in the twentieth century. Bruccoli's point about vagueness as a strategy in the novel had in fact often been noted by critics. One of its first readers, the novelist Edith Wharton, complained in a 1925 letter to Fitzgerald of the fact that we learn very little of Gatsby's character. He remains a shadowy figure for us: 'to make Gatsby really Great, you ought to have given us his early career . . . instead of a short résumé of it' (Wharton, 1925, p. 106). This same complaint had earlier been voiced by Fitzgerald's editor, Maxwell Perkins (Perkins, 1925, pp. 101–2). But it was essential for Fitzgerald's purposes, and for the sense of Gatsby as a mythic figure, that he should remain mysterious. Fitzgerald had written at some length about one telling incident from Gatsby's childhood, but then excluded the episode in order, he wrote, to preserve a 'sense of mystery' about him (Fitzgerald, 1963, p. 509). This excluded incident became the short story 'Absolution'.

The sense of mystery and rumour surrounding Gatsby is indeed well preserved in the novel. Nick Carraway tells us a great deal about Gatsby, so that we know the date and place of his birth, and something of the circumstances of his youth. But by a clever technique Fitzgerald at the same time indicates his essentially mysterious nature. This technique is especially evident at the beginning of Chapter 6. Carraway's ostensible task here is to relate the facts of Gatsby's life, in order to counter the rumours of his origins (p. 108). But the chapter actually adds to the sense of mystery, glamour and notoriety that attaches to Gatsby, since Carraway interlaces his factual narrative with repeated references to the rumours and to his own imaginative version of Gatsby. This strategy is most obvious in the following example. At first, Carraway offers something factual to the reader; Gatsby's parents 'were shiftless and unsuccessful farm people — his imagination had never really accepted them as his parents at all'. In the very next sequence, though, he shifts from the factual into adopting the mythic approach to Gatsby, in what is the most overt statement of Gatsby's status as a kind of god. 'Jay Gatsby of West Egg, Long Island, sprang from his Platonic conception of himself. He was a son of God' (p. 105).

There are several good reasons why Fitzgerald wished Gatsby to be mysterious. An obvious one is economy, which in turn is related to the requirement that the reader should not be allowed to become morally critical of Gatsby. It is essential that his bootlegging activities should not be particularly clear or prominent, otherwise the reader's sympathy for him, directed by Carraway, is likely to recede. But it has generally been accepted that Fitzgerald's main use of vagueness is to make Gatsby into a mythic figure.

The sentence about Gatsby being 'a son of God' is the most explicit reference to his mythic status. But the mystery of his origins is continually insisted upon; even Tom Buchanan describes him as 'Mr Nobody from Nowhere' (p. 136). When Gatsby's father appears in the final chapter, he is portrayed as an insignificant, bucolic figure, somewhat akin to the shepherd in Shakespeare's *A Winter's Tale* who finds and adopts the king's child. Further evidence for Gatsby's status is seen in his comment about Daisy's relation to Tom: 'it was just personal' (p. 158). Gatsby's own love for Daisy and his attempt to repeat the past are, then, much more than personal, individual desires. In fact, his quest is described as 'the following of a grail' (p. 155), and his waiting outside the Buchanan house is a sacred 'vigil' (p. 152). At one point Fitzgerald subtly suggests that Gatsby's powers are somehow superhuman. At the beginning of Chapter 3 the repetition of 'his' becomes almost a chorus to Gatsby's power of transforming the ordinary into the glittering (p. 45). Later in the same chapter, the moon is described as being 'produced like the supper, no doubt, out of a caterer's basket' (p. 49).

There are, of course, references to Gatsby's place in the American past; notably in the novel's final paragraphs, where Carraway evokes the Dutch sailors. In seeing America for the first time, they share Gatsby's wonder and innocence at the opportunities offered by America. J.F. Callahan writes that the October month of love which Daisy and Gatsby had shared is a reference to Columbus' discovery of America in October, and Gatsby's attempt to recapture that time is part of a cultural desire for a lost innocence (Callahan, 1972, p. 20). Critics also cite some of the supposedly 'sacramental' qualities of the novel: for example, Gatsby's shirts which he shows to Daisy (p. 99); the continual drinking in the novel; or the list of names of the people who come to Gatsby's house (pp. 67–9). Several critics have remarked that the list becomes a kind of epic catalogue, echoing lists of warriors or ships in the works of Homer and Xenephon (Eble, 1977, p. 89). However, it is an updated catalogue, referring specifically to the American situation and reflecting the diverse origins of the settlers who came to America. Another element of the novel reflecting myth is the presence of the owl-eyed man, the recurring figure who appears as one of the few mourners at Gatsby's funeral. The owl-eyed man, who is symbolically linked with the hoarding of the eyes of Dr T.J. Eckleburg, speaks Gatsby's epitaph, 'poor son-of-a-bitch' (p. 182). Several critics have suggested that this figure is reminiscent of the blind prophet Tiresias, who appears both in *Oedipus Rex* and T.S. Eliot's *The Waste Land*. Tiresias possesses tragic knowledge, and here the owl-eyed man is left as a commentator on the tragedy of Gatsby (see Lehan, 1966, p. 121).

If Gatsby's mythic status has not been difficult for critics to accept, then some debate has arisen over the meaning of the myth that *The Great Gatsby* supposedly represents. Marius Bewley writes that Gatsby is 'a creature of myth in whom is incarnated the aspiration and the ordeal of his race' (Bewley, 1954, pp. 43–4). The implication, generally shared by critics, is that Gatsby the mythic figure is an embodiment of certain American ideals and characteristics. He is implicitly linked to some of the other figures of American literature who have a similar status, in particular to James Fenimore Cooper's Natty Bumppo, and to Mark Twain's Huckleberry Finn. These characters are supposedly mythical in that they manifest abstract ideals attractive to Americans: personal freedom, a self-reliant individuality, a belief in personal integrity rather than conformity. It is useful here to recall Jacques Barzun's definition of mythical characters as those figures who, 'whether real or imaginary . . . express and embody destinies, aspirations, or attitudes' typical of individuals or races (Perosa, 1965, p. 73). In Fenimore Cooper's five novels which make up the Leatherstocking Tales (1823–41), Natty is a character of crucial importance. His need to preserve his personal integrity without compromise drives him always into the wilderness, away from the influence of the settlements. In *The Adventures of Huckleberry Finn* (1884), Huck's 'sound heart' triumphs over his socially formed conscience when he decides to assist the slave Jim in escaping from Miss Watson. At the end of the novel Huck decides to 'light out for the Territory', escaping the influences that would destroy his individuality and sense of self. His action has come to be considered an archetypal gesture in American literature.

Critics on *The Great Gatsby* have often placed Gatsby in this tradition of mythic figures. 'For although he is treated with more irony than they . . . he shares their ideal of innocence, escape, and the purely personal code of conduct' (Chase, 1957, p. 301). In noting that Fitzgerald treats the mythical stance ironically, though, Chase is suggesting an important point about *The Great Gatsby*: that if it is a myth of America, then it is about America's failure to live up to its stated ideals and to its past of frontier and pioneer. While Natty and Huck had a frontier or a 'territory' to which they could escape, Gatsby has nowhere; significantly in the novel, he moves from West to East, reversing the pattern of the pioneer and the settler, and thereby indicating that the dream of individual freedom from institutions and settlements is over.

These ideas are present in several ways in the novel, and are often subtly revealed to us. For example, the frontier and the Western tradition are both embodied in Dan Cody, the figure who made a protégé of the young Gatsby, and whose photograph still hangs in Gatsby's bedroom (p. 107). Cody's name is derived from two larger than life figures of American history: the pioneer Daniel Boone, and Bill Cody the Westerner. Cody is intended to be a latter-day reflection of these figures, and in adopting Gatsby, he passes on the values of freedom, exploration and opportunity. However, Cody himself is a figure in decline, with nowhere to explore. Having been part of the mining rushes since the 1870s, in the twentieth century he is the subject of 'turgid journalism' (p. 106), and his yacht circles aimlessly around the continent (p. 107). Carraway hints that Cody is an unattractive, violent, drunken character, an anachronism, the 'pioneer debauchee' who 'brought back to the Eastern seaboard the savage violence of the frontier brothel and saloon' (p. 107). Carraway manages to distinguish the qualities of Gatsby's dream from Cody's behaviour, but throughout the novel he retains an ironic attitude towards the relevance of the pioneer spirit to contemporary American society.

Thus, Fitzgerald's myth seems to be about the decadence of American values, and the evidence for Fitzgerald's deliberate references to American culture is very strong. At the last minute Fitzgerald thought of changing the title to 'Under the Red White and Blue', cabling Perkins to this effect. He seems to have refrained only because there was just a fortnight to publication and it was probably too late for a change (Mizener, 1951, p. 171). However, the final effect of the novel's mythic status has been much debated; I will discuss it further below, in sections on the theme of America in the novel, and on the character of Gatsby. Is *The Great Gatsby* an attack on the loss of American values? Is Gatsby a tragic figure, or does he gain a kind of triumph in the novel?

The Non-American myth

It was noted above that while there was a great deal of critical consensus about the mythic elements of *The Great Gatsby*, there was some debate about the kind of myth Fitzgerald was writing. Several critics have maintained that although the novel is very much about specifically American themes, the kind of myth it embodies is much more universal. In fact, this was one of the points I noted above about the use of myth by James Joyce and T.S. Eliot: that through it they attempted to convey the universality of myth, rather than limit significance and relevance to one particular time and place. Several of the elements cited above as evidence of *The Great Gatsby*'s mythic status are not relevant to American themes alone. For example, if the owl-eyed man is Tiresias, then he indicates that Gatsby's tragedy can be considered as universal as that of Oedipus. *The Great Gatsby* can be read as a myth of lost innocence. Gatsby, the tragic hero, has maintained an innocent capacity to wonder, and a belief in the ability to recapture past time. His tragedy is that this innocence makes him a victim of others, and that the belief in recovering time is an illusion. This view has often been stated by critics; for example, 'Gatsby's essential incorruptibility is heroic' (Mizener, 1951, p. 177). Mizener defines the novel as 'tragic pastoral' (Mizener, 1951, p. 175), an insight developed intelligently by Sergio Perosa in a chapter with that title (Perosa, 1965, pp. 52–82).

Thus, for some critics, *The Great Gatsby* is about a general human predicament, in spite of its setting in American culture and references to American history. Gatsby's dream, although it finally destroys him tragically, raises him above the other characters, giving him, as Carraway finally recognizes, a dignity and worth that the other characters have never possessed. Almost the last thing he says to Gatsby is 'You're worth the whole damn bunch put together' (p. 160). Put this way, Gatsby's dream is much more than a reflection of the American dream or belief in historical American ideals. It is a dream of 'unity, integration, cohesion between mind and matter, man and nature, the dream wherein one heightens the world' and thus not exclusively an American dream (Callahan, 1972, p. 11). Kenneth Eble states that *The Great Gatsby* represents 'Fitzgerald's attempt to capture the essential truth of the romantic vision' (Eble, 1977, p. 94).

One of the critics to pursue this argument at length is Richard Lehan, in his book *F. Scott Fitzgerald and the Craft of Fiction*. Using the facts about Fitzgerald's love of the Romantic poets, in particular Keats, Lehan argues that much of Fitzgerald's work is about the survival of Romantic values in the modern age. Lehan specifically considers the relation between time in Romantic thought and the themes of *The Great Gatsby*. Gatsby is related to the other Fitzgerald characters such as Dick Diver in *Tender is the Night* and Monroe Stahr in *The Last Tycoon*, who possess vision, but are destroyed by those who act against their idealism; by Tom Buchanan, in the case of Gatsby. While acknowledging the evidence that *The Great Gatsby* was intended to be a novel about America, Lehan points out that for Fitzgerald, the American dream was something he approached on an individual and personal level. We unnecessarily limit *The Great Gatsby* if we consider it only a novel about America, since Fitzgerald 'extended his novel beyond history to the realm of metaphysics, to the story of man's fight against the process of time . . . the hidden enemy . . . is time itself' (Lehan, 1966, p. 116). Lehan would grant mythic status to Gatsby, but sees his heroism in his attempt to defy time. Even Gatsby's move from West to East is not necessarily the ironic reversal of frontier, as other critics have argued, but evidence for Gatsby's defiance of time, an attempt to reverse the path of the sun (Lehan, 1966, p. 119).

Lehan's idea about Gatsby's attempt to reverse the process of time refers back to the much quoted dialogue between Gatsby and Carraway in Chapter 6. Carraway states that Gatsby should not expect too much of Daisy; that circumstances have changed her from the woman she was five years ago, and 'You can't repeat the past'. Gatsby's reply, 'Can't repeat the past? . . . Why of course you can!' (p. 117), is often considered one of the most revealing moments in the novel. For Lehan, it makes Gatsby into a hero confronting the universal human issue of loss and past time, a metaphysical adventurer. As I shall later discuss, time is crucial in the novel, and Gatsby is defeated by its inevitable progress as much as he is defeated by Buchanan.

I shall conclude this section by quoting another of the parts of *The Great Gatsby* which can be used as evidence either for the novel's examination of American myth, or for its consideration of Romanticism. At the end of Chapter 6, when Gatsby has told of his affair with Daisy, Carraway imagines a rhythm behind Gatsby's actual words. Even as he condemns Gatsby's 'appalling sentimentality', the words remind him of something in the past:

> Through all he said, even through his appalling sentimentality, I was reminded of something — an elusive rhythm, a fragment of lost words, that I had heard somewhere a long time ago. For a moment a phrase tried to take shape in my mouth and my lips parted like a dumb man's, as though there was more struggling upon them than a wisp of startled air. But they made no sound, and what I had almost remembered was uncommunicable for ever. (p. 118).

For critics who see primarily the American theme of the novel, the lost words here would be the American Declaration of Independence, and Carraway's inability to recall the words indicates his own lost innocence. But, given the particular context of Gatsby's love for Daisy, one could equally see that Carraway's lost rhythms are that of some poem, probably Romantic, and possibly Keats' s 'Ode to a Nightingale'. In either case, the issue of the novel as myth seems to be confirmed by such a paragraph, while not being decisively closed by it.

The Formalist Approach

Formalism may be defined as a critical approach in which the text under discussion is considered primarily as a structure of words. That is, the main focus is on the arrangement of language, rather than on the implications of the words, or on the biographical and historical relevance of the work in question. A strictly formalist critic would, for example, approach *The Great Gatsby* as a structure of words, ignoring the details of Fitzgerald's life and the social and historical contexts of the novel. However, formalism, or the concept of strict literary formalism, has often been attacked by individual literary critics or schools of criticism on the grounds that it reduces the text to nothing more than a series of words, thereby limiting its meaning and power. It is true that the Russian Formalists in the early years of the century attempted to examine the text in this way, but Western formalist approaches have tended to be much less theoretical. In practice, such critics have been very responsible to the meaning and themes of the work in question, rather than adopting a linguistic approach. For example, from the 1930s onwards, a movement in Britain and America, loosely called the 'New Criticism' began to dominate critical activity and teaching methods. The New Critics have been called formalist, but this is true only in one sense. They certainly returned the focus to the text, in reaction to the dominant biographical and historical criticism of the time. But at their best, the New Critics demonstrated the complex inter-relation between the arrangement, connotation, and ambiguity of the words on the page to the human themes those words explored. It is no accident that critical interest in *The Great Gatsby* was stimulated most during the 1940s and 1950s, when the New Criticism was a dominant teaching and research practice. This approach encouraged identification of theme and meaning (unlike a strictly formalist approach), so long as such insights were carefully grounded in the text, and not deriving from any evidence outside of it. For example, they would mistrust any critical approach in which evidence came primarily from knowledge of what the writer intended, or from the emotional impressions of the reader. Such approaches were named, respectively, the 'intentional' and the 'affective' fallacy (see Wimsatt and Beardsley, 1954). What mattered were the words on the page in front of us, to be scrutinized as carefully as possible.

In theory at least, New Critical formalist critics would mistrust a view of *The Great Gatsby* which emphasized the socio-historical implications of the novel, since these are, strictly, outside the range of their approach. But one of the features of *The Great Gatsby* noted above is that it has usually been approached as a novel about America, and a systematic, or even attentive reading of the words on the page would probably endorse this conclusion. Critics on *The Great Gatsby* have almost always linked insight into technique to some larger insight about the themes and meanings of the novel. A formalist critic might examine *The Great Gatsby* in a number of ways; through the recurring images or symbols; through the repetition of words or phrases; through the technical aspects of the novel, such as the disruption of narrative chronology, or the relevance of point of view. But even an emphasis on *The Great Gatsby* as a piece of craftsmanship has usually resulted in some statement increasing appreciation of the themes of the novel.

'The Great Gatsby' as craft

'The novel is a work of genius, but it is equally a triumph of craftsmanship' (Bruccoli, 1985, p. 2). By now, this is a fairly well established view, but contemporary reviewers of *The Great Gatsby*, and some later critics, have expressed astonishment at the development shown by Fitzgerald after his earlier work. 'There is still a mystery about how everything came together for Fitzgerald . . . and about how it is such a great advance over *This Side of Paradise* and *The Beautiful and Damned*' (Eble, 1977, no page). These first two novels of Fitzgerald, dated 1920 and 1922 respectively, were remarkably popular, but in terms of mature technique and characterization, they are far below the level of achievement of *The Great Gatsby*. They prompted Fitzgerald's friend Edmund Wilson to write of him, in 1922, 'he has been given imagination without intellectual control of it; he has been given a desire for beauty without an aesthetic ideal; and he has been given a gift for expression without many ideas to express' (Wilson, 1922, p. 22). As a criticism of the earlier novels, this is a valid point expressed in a memorable way. But it is quite irrelevant to *The Great Gatsby*. Furthermore, recent evaluations of the two novels which preceded it have emphasized not the immaturity they apparently embody, but the deliberate methods that Fitzgerald was pursuing in them; methods he was drastically to alter for *The Great Gatsby*.

James E. Miller's much quoted study of Fitzgerald's craft, *F. Scott Fitzgerald: His Art and his Technique*, is important in the identification of the conscious influences that Fitzgerald chose, and stimulating in examining the implications of those choices. Miller demonstrates that Fitzgerald is a much more intelligent and self-conscious writer than had hitherto been acknowledged, and shows how he developed from writing novels of 'saturation' to the novel of 'selection'. *The Great Gatsby* represents Fitzgerald's rejection of the saturation novel in favour of selection, and it sets the scene for the work which follows.

Briefly, the novel of saturation was the result of a technique used by H. G. Wells, an important early influence on Fitzgerald. Such a novel would attempt to be inclusive, and its value would lie in the range of included material, since its object was to reflect the character of the author and the complexities of the age. In the early years of the century a debate began between Wells and Henry James, James attacking Wells and arguing for the novel of selection. The author must show intellectual control over the material, and aim for the novel being an impression of life. Having established this opposition, Miller goes on to demonstrate how it applies to Fitzgerald. *This Side of Paradise* was a novel of saturation, written under the influence of Wells's side of the debate, and also under the influence of Compton McKenzie. Miller sees *The Beautiful and Damned* as a transitional and unsuccessful work. Though still in the saturation school, Fitzgerald was developing a more sophisticated use of selection and point of view. *The Great Gatsby* represents Fitzgerald's emergence into the selection school, being influenced particularly by his reading of Joseph Conrad, whom James had cited as an example of a selective author. Fitzgerald's reading of and admiration for Conrad are well documented in the letters, and elsewhere he called *Nostromo* 'the greatest novel since "Vanity Fair"' (Mizener, 1951, p. 336n). In his 'Introduction' to the 1934 reissue of *The Great Gatsby*, Fitzgerald said that when writing the novel he had recently reread Conrad's 'Preface' to *The Nigger of the Narcissus* (Fitzgerald, 1934, p. 109). There, Conrad writes that the novelist must attempt 'perfect blending of form and substance', a 'care for the shape and ring of sentences'. Only when these are achieved can the writer achieve 'the light of magic suggestiveness . . . brought to play for an evanescent instant over the commonplace surface of words' (Conrad, 1897, pp. 13–14). Critics usually agree that in *The Great Gatsby* Fitzgerald followed this advice, and achieved the 'magic suggestiveness' of language. This meant a great deal of work; the novel took about three years to complete, though not all of Fitzgerald's energies during this period went into it. Changes and revisions were made right up until the last minute: Fitzgerald had warned his editor that proof revision would be one of the most expensive affairs since *Madame Bovary* (Fitzgerald, 1963, p. 172). Incidentally, the famous symbol in the novel, the eyes of Dr T.J. Eckleburg, was not added until the proof stage. Fitzgerald saw a proposed design for the novel's dust jacket, an illustration with two eyes over a fairground scene, and, struck by the concept, revised the novel to include the symbol (see Mizener, 1972, p. 70).

In part, the labour over *The Great Gatsby* and the revisions to the proof were to do with the structure of the novel. Fitzgerald revised continually as regards the placing of different scenes; for example, what are now the much-praised final paragraphs of the novel originally appeared at the end of Chapter 1. In part, as noted in the section on myth, Fitzgerald's intention in disrupting the chronological telling of Gatsby's past was to provide a sense of mystery about him. The arrangement also gives some suspense to the novel. In his study, Miller demonstrates how we learn gradually about Gatsby. He usefully quotes Ford Madox Ford's book on collaborating with Conrad, and how they jointly decided that in order to imitate life, the straightforward telling of a story was not good enough: 'It became very early evident to us that what was the matter with the novel . . . was that it went straight forward, whereas in your gradual making acquaintanceship with your fellows you never do go straight forward' (Miller, 1967, p. 112). Neither does our 'acquaintanceship' with Gatsby. After the first meeting at Gatsby's party (which is not until almost a third of the way into the book), we receive various versions of his past at different times, and only at the end is there built up a sense of sequence to his life. Miller demonstrates the technique thus:

> Allowing X to stand for the straight chronological account of the summer of 1922, and A, B, C, D, and E to represent the significant events of Gatsby's past, the nine chapters of *The Great Gatsby* may be charted: X, X, X, XCX, X, XBXCX, X, XCXDX, XEXAX. (Miller, 1967, p. 114).

Again, as noted above, Miller's structural analysis is not some dry formal exercise; it helps greatly in critical appreciation of the relation between Fitzgerald's art and the themes of the novel.

Point of View

While the character of Nick Carraway will be discussed later, the implications of his narrative point of view have been much debated by critics. To give a perspective to this subject, it is important to consider the question of Carraway's authority with regard to what he tells us, and also the nature of his own character which inevitably shapes his attitude to the story.

Critics were from the start perceptive about the advance in technical sophistication which *The Great Gatsby* represented in Fitzgerald's work. In *This Side of Paradise* and *The Beautiful and Damned*, the narrative point of view chosen made little or no distinction between the narrator and the central figure of the novel. Critics felt that the success of *The Great Gatsby* lay partly in the distance Fitzgerald was able to place between himself and Gatsby. Some have indeed suggested that Carraway and Gatsby represent two parts of Fitzgerald himself:

> In the earlier books author and hero tended to melt into one because there was no internal principle of differentiation by which they might be separated . . . But in *Gatsby* is achieved a dissociation, by which Fitzgerald was able to isolate one part of himself, the spectatorial or aesthetic [from] . . . the dream-ridden romantic adolescent. (Troy, 1945, pp. 225–6).

Carraway is the comparatively timid, mildly cynical, tolerant yet moralistic observer whose rather snobbish alertness to class distinction is announced on the very first page. Most critics have regarded him as a brilliantly apt narrator, because of his ability to be involved in scenes yet objectively distant about them. He makes a telling comment about himself when he says that he is 'within and without, simultaneously enchanted and repelled by the inexhaustible variety of life' (p. 42). The ability to be both 'within and without' qualifies Carraway as narrator; he is 'within' and thus close to the actions he describes, yet simultaneously 'without' and able to be objective about them. His instinct to judge people is balanced by his tolerance of them, and he prides himself on his 'honesty'. Perosa writes that the opening pages define Carraway as 'the *perfect* narrator' (Perosa, 1965, p. 62).

While these are the qualities which commend Carraway, other critics have not been so sure about his supposed perfection. In part, this uncertainty about Carraway's authority derives from recognition of the sophisticated use of the flawed point of view made by Henry James and Ford Madox Ford, who along with Conrad, best exemplified the 'novel as selection' side of the debate with Wells. In James's extraordinary tale, 'The Turn of the Screw' (1898), we are given a governess's account of her relations with two children. Gradually she suspects that the bodies of the children are being possessed by a pair of dead lovers who had previously occupied the house. However, the reader also comes to suspect that the governess herself is obsessed with the dead lovers, and that she has repressed sexual feelings for the children's father. At this point, the reader sees that the unbalanced governess is an untrustworthy narrator, and a woman whose actions place the lives of the children in danger. A similar technique is used in Ford Madox Ford's novel *The Good Soldier* (1915). The narrator, Dowell, resembles Carraway to some extent. In the novel, he is cruelly deceived by a number of people supposedly intimate with him, and the reader begins to see the significance of events to which Dowell is blind. We realize the deceptions practiced upon him before his narrative explicitly reveals them to us.

Although these are extreme examples of both the novel of selection and the device of flawed narrator, their closeness to the style and techniques of *The Great Gatsby* make critical comparisons possible, opening up a debate on Carraway as flawed narrator. R.W. Stallman attacks the idea that Nick has moral authority, and argues that this is acceptable only to the 'duped' reader (Stallman, 1961, p. 137). Other critics as well as Stallman have pointed out that Nick's supposed honesty must be questioned, as it is broken down in the novel, and Nick becomes a morally 'ambivalent' narrator (Stallman, 1961, p. 134; see also Scrimgeour, 1966). The attraction which Nick feels toward Gatsby also affects the narrative, resulting in the bias that he shows. As noted above, Nick is cautious, polite, circumspect, and is undoubtedly attracted, though not at first, to the reckless, single-minded ambition of Gatsby the self-made man. In fact, part of Fitzgerald's narrative strategy is to have Carraway lend dignity, depth and cultural relevance to Gatsby. This can be seen in Chapter 8, when Carraway tells the story of Gatsby's meeting and subsequent affair with Daisy (p. 154ff). The words used are clearly not those of Gatsby; the bare facts are there, but presented in a way to give them an aura of romance, dignity, and 'ripe mystery' (p. 154). One could contrast the style here with Gatsby's own crude deception about the origins of his wealth (pp. 71–3).

Narrative

Another of the technical qualities of *The Great Gatsby* related to point of view is the variety of sources Carraway uses for the narration. While Fitzgerald actually furnishes us with an account of Gatsby from childhood, this is not only broken up in the narrative, as noted above, but also derives from different sources. Incidents from Gatsby's childhood are given by Gatsby's father. The story of Gatsby's adolescence, adoption by Dan Cody, meeting with Daisy, and war experience is given by Gatsby himself, while Daisy's point of view is supplied by Jordan. Wolfsheim gives an account of Gatsby after the war and of his rise in bootlegging, bringing Nick up to the time that his own narrative begins. Further, Nick works on different narratives in order to fill in the gaps in his own knowledge. For example, in his account of the killing of Myrtle Wilson, he obviously has adapted the evidence given by Michaelis, the principal witness at the inquest. The language becomes appropriate to that used in the court of law, with its precision concerning time and identity of witnesses (p. 142ff). This narrative, though, is broken up whenever Nick can return to events at which he himself was present. The narrative relying on Michaelis' evidence is interrupted when Nick, Tom and Jordan arrive at the accident scene (p. 144). After some eighteen pages, the evidence is used once more to fill in the gaps of what has happened (p. 162).

One of the effects of this shifting in styles and sources is to add a certain authenticity to the narrative at the points where Nick must write of something he did not experience. Another effect is to preserve some of the mystery that is essential to the novel; though Fitzgerald also adds suspense through the method chosen. For example, the reader learns about Gatsby only gradually. Furthermore, there is a suspense created about the very events of the novel. After reading that Tom's car is being driven 'toward death' and then that there has been an inquest (p. 142), the reader is keen to read on. In fact, an astute reader might start to wonder why Michaelis, rather than Wilson, Gatsby or Daisy, is the principal witness at the inquest.

Symbolism

While hardly any discussion of *The Great Gatsby* would be complete without consideration of Fitzgerald's symbols, it is interesting that there has been no hard and fast critical consensus on their exact meaning. In fact, critics with elaborate schemes of meaning often seem to be inviting disagreement, as exceptions can be found to test the invented hypotheses. For example, André Le Vot examines colour symbolism in the novel, in particular the way that yellow and blue are associated with Gatsby. He argues that Gatsby's inner, private self, is symbolized by blue (his blue lawns, the livery of his servants), with its connotations of remoteness and coldness. The self which Gatsby wants to present to the world is symbolized by yellow (his station wagon and the 'death car' are yellow, his cocktail music is also described as yellow), suggesting gaiety, wealth and community (Le Vot, 1984, p. 145). The weakness of Le Vot's system is that it is too schematic, and there are examples of yellow and blue which do nothing to support the scheme. Jordan Baker and Daisy's daughter both have yellow hair (pp. 24, 123). Eckleburg's spectacles and Wilson's garage are yellow (pp. 29, 30), two women in yellow dresses recur in Chapter 3, and a yellow trolley follows Gatsby's train as he leaves Louisville (p. 159). It would be difficult to fit these instances into Le Vot's colour scheme, as well as the fact that Tom's coupé is blue (p. 147).

In part, the point is that the kinds of symbols in *The Great Gatsby* are suggestive rather than definite, and that their power accordingly lies in their suggestiveness. Critics often point out associations between the symbols and those used by T.S. Eliot in *The Waste Land*. The most obvious is the 'valley of ashes' between West Egg and New York, reminiscent of the Waste Land itself, and there are other echoes of Eliot's poetry. Some features of Eliot's poem, 'The Hollow Men' (1925) are echoed in *The Great Gatsby*. In the poem, the hollow men (with heads 'filled with straw') inhabit a valley. The adjective 'hollow' recurs in connection with Wilson, another inhabitant of a valley, while Tom is a 'straw-haired man'

(p. 13), and Nick and Gatsby both wear straw hats (p. 121). Again, these are Fitzgerald's suggestive images, and their power remains in their suggestiveness rather than in their definite meaning.

Perhaps the most celebrated single symbol in the novel is the advertisement hoarding of the eyes of Dr T.J. Eckleburg, though, as noted above, the eyes at first played no part in the novel. It is not easy to pin down the exact meaning of the eyes, though a general critical consensus seems to be that they suggest the modern world's loss of God, or a spiritual dimension. Because of this loss, they simply brood gloomily over the chaotic waste land. One critic has seen the eyes as 'the image of an impotent god' (Perosa, 1965, p. 79), while another sees them as representing 'some kind of detached intellect . . . presiding fatalistically over the little tragedy' (Miller, 1967, p. 125).

To some extent the eyes are a powerful symbol precisely because no definite, absolute meaning can successfully be assigned to them, keeping their possible meanings always alive for the reader. With such a technique, Fitzgerald had fulfilled the prescription of Conrad that he so admired; that the writer should aim for 'the light of magic suggestiveness . . . brought to play for an evanescent instant over the commonplace surface of words' (Conrad, 1897, pp. 13–14).

The Authorial Perspective

The place of 'The Great Gatsby' in Fitzgerald's other works

As mentioned above, the New Criticism was a movement emphasizing that the text in front of us was the primary focus of attention, and that insights available from secondary or other sources should be used minimally. However, in the case of Fitzgerald and *The Great Gatsby*, the situation is not so simple. The themes and, indeed, something of the basic story of *The Great Gatsby*, had been already explored by Fitzgerald in other works, and he was to explore them after 1925. Almost all extended criticism of *The Great Gatsby* has included a section on these relevant works, as critics recognize the valuable perspective that they can provide on the novel. In particular, the relevance of the short stories 'The Diamond as Big as the Ritz' (1922), 'Winter

Dreams' (1922), ' "The Sensible Thing" ' (1924, 'Absolution' (1924) and 'The Rich Boy' (1926) has been debated. These are the stories most often cited by critics on *The Great Gatsby*, in the belief that in them Fitzgerald was working through the themes he was to deal with in the novel.

One of the persistent attitudes to Fitzgerald is that his short stories were written carelessly, hastily, and purely for the large financial rewards they returned from fashionable magazines. While some of Fitzgerald's own comments can be used to support these views, it would be a mistake to underestimate the stories. They are much more than formula fiction, and they repay close reading. In them, Fitzgerald was often working out ideas that he would develop further in the novels and, at their best, they stand by themselves as achievements. Also, the stories are often barely disguised transformations of events and incidents in Fitzgerald's own life. Since one of these is especially relevant to understanding this group of stories, and has implications for our appreciation of *The Great Gatsby*, it should briefly be related here.

In 1918 Fitzgerald, aged twenty one, was in the army and stationed near Montgomery, Alabama. While there, he fell in love with a local woman, Zelda Sayre, and they became engaged. After demobilization, however, Fitzgerald in New York found it difficult to get a well paid job, and Zelda broke off their engagement. However, in 1919, when Fitzgerald's first novel, *This Side of Paradise*, was accepted for publication, she renewed it. The series of events played a large part in Fitzgerald's imagination and in his fiction. Of course, there are correspondences with *The Great Gatsby*, though whereas Gatsby had lost Daisy, Fitzgerald both lost and regained Zelda. The themes Fitzgerald located in this incident, though, became much more complex than the anecdotal. He felt that it influenced his attitudes towards success, towards loss, and towards the rich, and these attitudes again appear in *The Great Gatsby*. As late as 1936 Fitzgerald was brooding on the meanings of the incident:

It was one of those tragic loves doomed for lack of money, and one day the girl closed it out on the basis of common sense. During a long summer of despair I wrote a novel instead of letters, so it came out all right, but it came out all right for a different person. (Fitzgerald, 1974, p. 47).

'Winter Dreams' and '"The Sensible Thing"'

Both of these may be considered early versions of *The Great Gatsby*, in which Fitzgerald explores again the relation between love and money; the relation he had seen in the story of his engagement and re-engagement to Zelda Sayre. In 'Winter Dreams' Dexter Green, aged about fourteen, becomes infatuated with the eleven-year-old heiress Judy Jones. There is a class difference between the two, as in *The Great Gatsby*, but in the course of the story Dexter becomes an astute business man, and builds up wealth. At twenty-four, he reckons to be making more money than any man his age in the Northwest (Fitzgerald, 1987, p. 373). Although Judy flirts with him, Dexter is exasperated with her, and their affair comes to nothing. At the end of the story, Dexter, successful now in New York and aged thirty-two, chances to hear about Judy's marriage, and that her looks are fading. He is upset, not so much for Judy, but for the passage of time. That is, his dream concerning Judy was a dream of youth untouched by time, but the dream now proves illusory. Everything is 'left behind in the country of illusion, of youth . . . where his winter dreams had flourished' (Fitzgerald, 1987, p. 383).

The story's real focus is not particularly on Judy at all, except in that she is an emblem of Dexter's romantic belief that youth and beauty will not fade. There are obvious resemblances here to Gatsby's relation with Daisy. As with Dexter, Gatsby's illusion is emphasized more than the object of love; we can see the similarity to Gatsby's comment that the love of Tom and Daisy was 'just personal'. In 'Winter Dreams' Dexter's dream is undoubtedly over, and the story is about the break-up of his romantic illusions concerning youth and beauty. The final emphasis is on loss: 'long ago, there was something in me, but now that thing is gone . . . I cannot cry. I cannot care. That thing will come back no more' (Fitzgerald, 1987, p. 384). In *The Great Gatsby* the loss of Gatsby's dream is much more ambiguous and complex; 'Winter Dreams' is a comparatively crude story, but it does allow us to understand Gatsby a little more fully.

'"The Sensible Thing"' is a finer story than 'Winter Dreams', in that there is more richness and ambiguity regarding the loss of the dream. In the story, which is strongly autobiographical, George O'Kelly is rejected by his fiancée, Jonquil Cary, on the grounds that he is too poor. Breaking off their engagement is more 'sensible' than marrying. However, a year later, after a period in Peru, O'Kelly arrives back in the USA. By now he is financially secure, and in 'a position of unlimited opportunity' (Fitzgerald, 1987, p. 393). Jonquil accepts him. In terms of formula fiction, this seems a perfectly conventional ending. But the true ending is more subtle, being about the loss of George's spontaneous love for Jonquil:

> He might press her close now till the muscles knotted on his arms — she was something desirable and rare that he had fought for and made his own — but never again an intangible whisper in the dusk, or on the breeze of night . . . There are all kinds of love in the world, but never the same love twice. (Fitzgerald, 1987, p. 397).

The moment is strongly similar to that in *The Great Gatsby*, when Carraway senses that Gatsby, having regained Daisy (whose names echoes 'Jonquil'), is also disillusioned:

> There must have been moments even that afternoon when Daisy tumbled short of his dreams — not through her own fault, but because of the colossal vitality of his illusion. It had gone beyond her, beyond everything. (pp. 102–3).

Like O'Kelly, Gatsby has lost the spontaneous freshness of love, which both men had hoped to recapture. Although by no means as complex as *The Great Gatsby*, there is an interesting irony in '"The Sensible Thing"'. Although O'Kelly is reunited with his lover, he has still lost his youthful view of the world, in much the same way that Fitzgerald saw himself as a 'different person' after the reunion with Zelda (Fitzgerald, 1974, p. 47). The dream of union had grown to be more important than the actual union.

While these two stories are important introductions to aspects of *The Great Gatsby*, critics are generally agreed that they are comparatively unsophisticated as prologues. It is important also not to misuse these stories. They provide a perspective on only one aspect of Gatsby; the relation between his dream and Daisy, rather than on the novel as a whole. The stories lack the sophistication of *The Great Gatsby*, not only at the thematic level, but in terms of narrative point of view, technical subtlety and memorability of phrasing. Above all, as Perosa warns, in relation to *The Great Gatsby*, these stories should be used for clarification only; otherwise, they could 'predispose or condition our interpretation of the novel from an all-too-narrow point of view' (Perosa, 1965, p. 58).

'The Diamond as Big as the Ritz' and 'The Rich Boy'

Although these stories were published four years apart, they both examine the effects of wealth on individuals; 'The Diamond as Big as the Ritz' does so in a fantastic manner, while 'The Rich Boy' does so realistically. Both have implications for an approach to *The Great Gatsby*, which itself can be considered a novel about wealth.

In the extract from 'The Crack-Up' quoted above, Fitzgerald considered the difference between himself as the man rejected by Zelda and the man who was once again accepted by her. In the same essay, he goes on to discuss the difference in attitude which this experience entailed:

> The man with the jingle of money in his pocket who married the girl a year later would always cherish an abiding distrust, an animosity, toward the leisure class. (Fitzgerald, 1974, p. 47).

This is far from the Fitzgerald who supposedly idealized and idolized the rich. It could be pointed out that Fitzgerald is writing this during the mid-1930s, at a time of great personal despair and bitterness. But this attitude of distrust towards the 'very rich' is present much earlier, both in these two stories and in *The Great Gatsby*.

In 'The Diamond as Big as the Ritz' John T. Unger, a middle-class boy from the mid-West at school in the East, befriends Percy Washington. Percy invites him to the family home in Montana for the summer vacation. On the train, he confides to Unger that the family possession is 'a diamond bigger than the Ritz-Carlton Hotel' (Fitzgerald, 1987, p. 76). It turns out that the Washington family home is built on a mountain which is a diamond, accidentally discovered by Fitz-Norman Culpepper Washington after the Civil War. He sold some of the diamonds, and built a secret estate, using the labour of slaves who never learned that slavery had been abolished. Although living in luxury, the Washingtons also live in fear that their mountain will be discovered. Unger falls in love with Percy's sister Kismine. However, she accidentally lets him know that their guests have to be killed when their vacation is over, for fear they will let slip the secret of the mountain. One night shortly after this revelation, aeroplanes appear over the château and a battle begins. In the chaos, Unger rescues Kismine and her sister, and they hurry to the mountain. While there, they see Percy's father, Braddock Washington, trying to bribe God. When this fails, the other Washingtons retreat into the mountain and blow it up. Unger and the two sisters survive, but the story ends with Unger disillusioned, left with Kismine but with no wealth and no prospects.

The story is a fantastic parable about wealth. The Washingtons are comically corrupted by their wealth, and their insecurity about it has led to inhuman actions: the keeping of the slaves and the murdering of the guests. In *The Great Gatsby*, Tom's speech about *The Rise of the Coloured Empires* (pp. 19–20) marks him as a realistic character somewhat analogous to the caricatured Washingtons. While 'The Diamond as Big as the Ritz' is about the attractions of wealth (the importance of the naïve Unger's viewpoint is crucial here), it morally reinforces the idea that wealth fails (as it failed for Dexter Green and George O'Kelly) to preserve beauty or innocence, and cannot prevent the passage of time. Gatsby's failure is based on his refusal to accept the idea; he believes naïvely in the ability to recapture the past and believes that wealth can assist him in the ideal.

'Let me tell you about the very rich. They are different from you and me. They possess and enjoy early, and it does something to them' (Fitzgerald, 1987, p. 110). These famous lines from 'The Rich Boy' announce its theme, which is an exploration of the effects of wealth on one man, Anson Hunter. Hunter turns out to be a failure in terms of his emotional life. He is cut off from people because of his wealth, or rather, because of the feeling of superiority which it brings. Far from praising the wealthy, Fitzgerald's statement leads to the condemnation of Hunter.

His sense of natural superiority over others quickly becomes remoteness. His actions in the story display his character; he wishes to be loved and attended to by women, but has nothing to give them in return. As he grows older, he becomes increasingly conservative. His emotional immaturity is signalled by the 'boy' of the title. Hunter is not attacked in the story, but he is considered as a kind of victim of his wealth (Wolfe, 1982, p. 248). In *The Great Gatsby* Tom is similar to Anson, and when Nick shakes hands with him, he describes him as a child (p. 186).

'Absolution'

The perspective on *The Great Gatsby* lent by the preceding stories directly concerns either the theme of loss or the theme of wealth. But 'Absolution', often considered Fitzgerald's finest story, provides a far more complex perspective. The events of the story are less significant than the themes involved. Rudolph Miller, an eleven-year-old Roman Catholic boy with a domineering father, twice lies in confession. He then goes to visit the priest to confess again, but Father Schwartz, who is undergoing a spiritual crisis, loftily dismisses Rudolph's 'apostasy' and then goes on to talk in a way that the frightened boy cannot understand:

> go and see an amusement park . . . Go to one at night and stand a little way off from it in a dark place . . . You'll see a big wheel made of lights turning in the air, and a long slide shooting boats down into the water. A band playing somewhere, and a smell of peanuts — and everything will twinkle. But it won't remind you of anything, you see. It will all just hang out there in the night like a coloured balloon — like a big yellow lantern on a pole . . . But don't get up close . . . because if you do you'll only feel the heat and the sweat and the life. (Fitzgerald, 1987, pp. 410–11).

In effect the priest has told the boy to trust in imaginative vision, and not to be distracted from it by the perishable physicality of the world. He himself has not been able to maintain this, distracted as he is by the 'girls with yellow hair [who] walked sensuously along roads' (Fitzgerald, 1987, p. 411). But he senses that Rudolph possesses imagination and, in this cryptic fashion, urges him to keep it.

Rudolph is an imaginative boy in rebellion against his father. One of his beliefs is that he is not the son of his parents, and he has invented an alter ego for himself, the suave Blatchford Sarnemington (Fitzgerald, 1987, pp. 401, 402–3). Of course, he is an avatar of Gatsby, who, as James Gatz, had invented Jay Gatsby, and had 'never really accepted' that his parents were his at all (p. 105). Although he is baffled and frightened by the talk of Father Schwartz, Rudolph does understand him to some extent: 'underneath his terror he felt that his own inner convictions were confirmed. There was something ineffably gorgeous somewhere that had nothing to do with God' (Fitzgerald, 1987, p. 411).

Although 'Absolution' was intended as a prologue for *The Great Gatsby*, one can see why Fitzgerald decided to exclude it (Fitzgerald, 1963, p. 509). The story deprives Gatsby's character of some of the mystery and suspense that is so essential to the novel. Further, it posits too simple an explanation for his dream and his conduct: in the novel, Gatsby's ambition is far more complex than is suggested by the eleven-year-old Rudolph Miller. In spite of this, as critics have recognised, the story is important in an overall analysis of the character of Gatsby. Gatsby accepts the truth of the imagination and its primacy over fact, but fails because, as Father Schwartz had warned the boy, he becomes involved in the world, in the 'sweat' of life.

While the stories examined in this section have been much debated by critics, on the grounds that they illuminate aspects of *The Great Gatsby*, it is important not to over-emphasize this argument. By its nature, the short story lacks the exploration of character and extensive development of theme that are typical of the novel. In *The Great Gatsby*, Fitzgerald not only explored the issues of his theme much more deeply, but did so in ways that were technically more sophisticated and challenging.

The Socio-historical Approach

'The Great Gatsby' and American themes

So far, we have examined *The Great Gatsby* from several perspectives; the mythic, the formalist, and in the context made available from Fitzgerald's other work. As its name indicates, a socio–historical approach may be characterized as one by which the novel's themes are explored in relation to their social and historical context. The assumption behind this approach is that whatever its subject matter, the literary work in some way reflects the prevailing interests and ideas of the time in which it was written. This would be true even of a novel which itself dealt with few characters or hardly any 'society'. For example, one of the first novels — Daniel Defoe's *The Adventures of Robinson Crusoe* (1719) — even though it seems removed from a social context actually reflects many of the ideas and concerns of Defoe's contemporary society. In particular, the novel endorses the contemporary rise of the middle class, by celebrating enterprise, rationality, and the capitalist spirit (Watt, 1957).

As mentioned above in the section on myth, *The Great Gatsby* can readily be considered a novel about American society at a particular moment, and this theme is more explicit than in Defoe's novel. Fitzgerald once wrote, 'I am interested in the individual only in his relation to society' (Callahan, 1972, p. 4). Various socio–historical approaches to *The Great Gatsby* are possible; critics have examined it as a novel about the 1920s, about the American character, or about the American past. Within these broad approaches a variety of attitudes is possible. The most basic has been to examine the novel as a comment on 'the American dream'.

Put simply, the American dream is the ideal of opportunity for all, of advancement in a career or society without regard to one's origin. The ideal was embodied in Jefferson's 'Declaration of Independence' as 'Life, Liberty, and the Pursuit of Happiness'. Jefferson was specifically reacting against the 'closed' European societies, where power and wealth were seen to be in the hands of an aristocratic governing elite.

> It has been a dream of being able to grow to fullest development as man and woman, unhampered by the barriers . . . erected in older civilizations, unrepressed by social orders which had developed for the benefit of classes rather than for the simple human being of any and every class. (Adams, 1932, p. 405).

Thus the dream idealizes those who are 'self-made', as opposed to those who gain wealth and status through inheritance. Naturally, in *The Great Gatsby*, Gatsby represents this self-made figure. In fact, the description of Gatsby as sprung 'from his Platonic conception of himself' is almost a comic exaggeration of the ideal.

As noted above, in the section on *The Great Gatsby* and myth, there has been some disagreement between critics who see it as primarily about the myths of America, and those who argue that the novel has a wider, even metaphysical relevance. However, even among those critics who agree that the novel is about the myths of America, there is a division. To put it simply, the debate is over whether Fitzgerald is showing the decline of the American dream in the twentieth century or whether he is suggesting that, from the beginning, the dream was an illusion.

'The withering of the American dream'

Although Fitzgerald is often represented as 'the spokesman for an age', suggesting that he somehow praised and celebrated the times of which he wrote, *The Great Gatsby* is in many respects a criticism of the 1920s. While this criticism is signalled in various ways, it is most notably apparent in the symbols and suggestiveness of the language used. The 'valley of ashes' suggests spiritual and moral sterility, and many more examples could be cited. Carraway, who is both attracted to and repelled by the East, at times reminds us of his isolation: 'I felt a haunting loneliness sometimes, and felt it in others — poor young clerks who loitered in front of windows waiting until it was time for a solitary restaurant dinner — young clerks in the dusk, wasting the most poignant moments of night and life' (p. 63). Boredom and loneliness are ever-present in the novel; Daisy is bored and (perhaps also to spite Tom) resumes her affair with Gatsby; Myrtle Wilson begins her affair out of frustration, and even Nick's affair with Jordan seems to have little to do with any mutual attraction. Fitzgerald also indicates the violence of the twenties. In fact, *The Great Gatsby* is quite a violent novel, in sharp contrast to Fitzgerald's preceding work. As well as the death of Myrtle, the murder of Gatsby and the suicide of Wilson, there is Tom's bloodying of Myrtle's nose, the chaotically violent behaviour of Gatsby's guests, and many reported acts of violence. These include Wolfsheim's story about the gangster murders and executions, reminders of Dan Cody's violent behaviour, and the violent ends of some of the people on the list of Gatsby's summer visitors (pp. 67–9). Death is repeatedly mentioned in the novel, and at different moments, appears in some guise; when Gatsby and Carraway go into New York, a hearse passes them (p. 75). Gatsby's car is described as the 'death car' (p. 144), and in an early draft of the novel, Carraway, seeing the car for the first time, thinks of a hearse (Piper, 1962, p. 331).

The critic George Garrett demonstrates a point that can easily be forgotten; that much of *The Great Gatsby* would have shocked its contemporary readers. The criminal negligence of Tom and Daisy goes unpunished, as do Tom's adulterous affairs (Garrett, 1985, p. 116). It would actually be quite easy for modern day readers not to realize that the novel is set during prohibition. Even though the bootlegging is an important feature of the novel, the way the characters drink and take drinking for granted tends to make the reader forget that most of the drinking is illegal. In *The Great Gatsby*, the twenties are not glamourized. The period is presented as a corrupt, amoral and violent time, in which loneliness, frustration and lost spiritual values are typical, and in which violent death is ever present. In this climate the American dream has undoubtedly 'withered' (Bewley, 1954, p. 37).

The Jeffersonian dream of a society open to all, and without barriers, is again contradicted by the events of the novel. The Buchanans represent a kind of wealthy aristocratic class in America, a class based on inherited money and the manners and attitudes that supposedly go with it. Naturally, they condescend towards the parvenu Gatsby, who, in spite of being 'self-made', and wealthy, lacks the manners and background which would allow him to belong to their leisure class. Tom's incredulity about Gatsby's having attended Oxford is summed up by reference to the ridiculous outfits Gatsby wears: 'An Oxford man! . . . Like hell he is! He wears a pink suit' (p. 128). In the eyes of the class Tom represents, Gatsby's parties are menageries and his car a 'circus wagon' (pp. 115, 127). Tom finally wins back Daisy not by appealing to her love but to her snobbery, by insinuating how Gatsby's means of making money has disqualified him from their class.

From this perspective, Fitzgerald examines the ways in which the American dream of equality and opportunity is contradicted by the rise of a leisure class who, with their estates, butlers and polo playing, ape the European aristocracy. It is worth pointing out that Gatsby himself recognizes this from the start. He 'takes' Daisy in the knowledge that he does not belong to her class, and the life story he first fabricates for Nick is an attempt to provide himself with a past suitable for the leisure class (pp. 154–5, 71–3).

From these examples, one could say that *The Great Gatsby* is about the closing of American society, and about twentieth-century developments which contradict and destroy the old American dream. The presence of Gatsby points back to the uncorrupted American dream, and he is also associated with the West and its promise. Although he is defeated, the dream gives Gatsby a dignity and a set of qualities lacking in the other characters. Carraway characterizes these as his optimism and openness to the promise of life. One of the first things Carraway tells us about Gatsby is that he has 'some heightened sensitivity to the promises of life' (p. 8). Nick knows that this quality, of believing in promises and in the future, is alien to himself and the people he has met in the East. Reflecting on his birthday, Nick too evokes promise, but in a way far different from Gatsby: 'Thirty — the promise of a decade of loneliness, a thinning list of single men to know, a thinning brief-case of enthusiasm, thinning hair' (p. 142).

Gatsby's hope and belief in promise make him somehow the embodiment of the abstract values of the American dream; and his violent death signals the end of that dream. For his elegy to Gatsby in the novel's final paragraphs, Carraway chooses to examine not Gatsby's personal past, but the past of America. He reflects on the moment of promise felt by the Dutch sailors seeing the continent for the first time, and finds an analogy with the spirit that inhabited Gatsby. The sailors become representative of humanity having 'for the last time' something that matches our 'capacity for wonder' (p. 188). This spirit of the newly discovered continent becomes the American dream, which in turn is reflected in Gatsby looking at the 'green light' on Daisy's dock. Carraway believes that Gatsby is heroic, in spite of all his reservations, because he finds in him the spirit of America he had considered lost. This idea twice becomes explicit, in the novel's final paragraphs, and when Gatsby talks about his love for Daisy: 'Through all he said . . . I was reminded of something — an elusive rhythm, a fragment of lost words, that I had heard somewhere a long time ago' (p. 118). The 'lost words' are the Declaration of Independence, and Gatsby's echo of them makes him the personal embodiment of their idealism.

Of course, Carraway also recognizes that the dream is part of history, not part of the present. The lost words here remain elusive to him, and in the closing paragraphs of the novel Carraway emphasizes that the dream was 'already behind him, somewhere back in that vast obscurity beyond the city, where the dark fields of the republic rolled on under the night' (p. 188). Cody is the corrupted twentieth-century version of the pioneer, while Meyer Wolfsheim represents the contemporary values of the East. Something of this same idea was already signified by Carraway's writing the names of Gatsby's guests on a schedule dated 5 July (p. 67). This is the day after Independence, ironically indicating that the cultural climate of the novel is after American idealism. *The Great Gatsby* becomes an American tragedy, but one in which Gatsby's heroism and idealism are constantly affirmed. As Bewley argues, '*The Great Gatsby* is a dramatic affirmation . . . of the American spirit in the midst of an American world that denies the soul. Gatsby exists in, and for, that affirmation alone' (Bewley, 1954, p. 52).

The Discredited Dream

These ideas about *The Great Gatsby* and the 'withering of the American dream' have become fairly standard, but they have also been seriously challenged by some critics. There are certain flaws in them, and in the kind of evidence offered in their support. For one thing, they depend largely upon accepting Carraway's evaluation of Gatsby. But since Carraway is a problem narrator, then his idealization cannot be accepted at face value. All of the positive values that come to be associated with Gatsby result from Carraway's version of the events, and from the addition of his own personal and cultural analysis. Without the gloss given to him, the story of Gatsby is merely that of a bootlegger killed by a garage owner. In part this is what Edith Wharton meant when she criticized Fitzgerald for not showing us where the greatness of Gatsby lay; without that perspective, the novel is not a tragedy but a 'fait divers' for the newspaper (Wharton, 1925, p. 106).

Several critics have gone to some lengths in demonstrating Carraway's unsuitability as a narrator, and these will be discussed further in the section on character. Here it needs only be stated that he 'camouflages' the truth at certain points (Stallman, 1961, p. 134), and that he admires Gatsby because of his own limitations. Thomas Hanzo points out how far Carraway and Gatsby are contrasting characters: Gatsby is rich, solitary, mysterious, obsessed and not bound by certain limits; Carraway is relatively poor, makes friends easily, is guarded in action and judgement (Hanzo, 1957, p. 62). But as well as being contrasts, these points can serve as the basis for why Gatsby's character is so attractive to Nick, and why his account of the summer's events makes a hero out of the bootlegger. Overall, recognition of Carraway's flaws has made critics wary of accepting Gatsby's heroism. Since this heroism is a crucial point in the argument that Gatsby is 'great' because he embodies the old American dream, it must lead to a revaluation of this idea.

The view that *The Great Gatsby* is about 'the withering of the American dream' also depends on a juxtaposition of past and present. The dream was once uncorrupted, and it is only in contemporary society that it has become 'withered'. An alternative view is that Fitzgerald criticizes the American dream as it has always existed, since it is an illusion that humans could never have fulfilled. Several kinds of evidence can be presented for this view: the use of the past in the novel, the kind of dream that Gatsby embodies, and the contrast between East and West.

The argument that *The Great Gatsby* concerns the recent corruption of the American dream relies upon a contrast in the novel between the uncorrupted past and the corrupt present. While it is clear that Carraway sees the present as corrupt and chaotic, several critics have attacked the argument that the past is somehow idealized. Dan Cody and Meyer Wolfsheim can be seen as degraded versions of the American dream — the 'debauched' version of the pioneer, and the gangster who fixed the World's Series. But both of them helped make Gatsby, and as such he could hardly be the current embodiment of the lasting purity of the dream. It is not even as though Gatsby has broken away from their influence; he is still closely allied to Wolfsheim, and he displays a photograph of Cody in his house. If they are the debauched version of the dream, then so is Gatsby. But another implication could be that the dream was always debauched. In reality, advancement always was in the hands of men like Cody and Wolfsheim.

The other past in the novel comes from Carraway's elegy for Gatsby, when he evokes the wonder of the Dutch sailors seeing the continent for the first time. But a close analysis of the language of the passage would suggest that it does not dignify Gatsby's dream very much. As Edwin Fussell writes, the passage insists that 'Gatsby's insatiable capacity for wonder could have, in the modern world, no proper objective' (Fussell, 1952, p. 253). That is, the sailors are seeing 'for the last time' something which would match the human capacity for wonder. Everything after that, Gatsby's dream as well as Jefferson's 'Declaration of Independence', would be illusion, false promise. The dream was indeed 'already behind' Gatsby and behind even Jefferson.

Some critics of *The Great Gatsby* have pointed out that there are really two American dreams. The one discussed so far is about the openness of society, and the freedom from institutions. In fact, much American writing is about the insistence upon this freedom, which, in the writings of Emerson, embodies also spiritual freedom. The other dream, however, is materialistic, and is concerned with material advancement in society. It is represented by Benjamin Franklin more than by any other single figure. One critic argues that *The Great Gatsby* is about the conflict between these two dreams (Barbour, 1973, p. 298). Gatsby's failure would thus be that in aiming for the ideal of equality and freedom, the ideal became confused with the mere making of money. But a more forceful criticism is that the dream of spiritual freedom is in fact inseparable from that of material advancement, and that in American history, the two became confused (Fussell, 1952, pp. 245–7).

An important point here is that the two are confused in Gatsby himself. Although he dreams of spiritual reunion with Daisy, his prior dream was of wealth and advancement, as is evident from the schedule of exercises and resolutions that he wrote in 1906 (pp. 179–80). The schedule is an echo of typical Benjamin Franklin resolves concerning thrift, health and the goal of advancement. The meeting, affair, loss and subsequent dream of regaining Daisy all happen eleven years later. Even Gatsby as a 'son of God' is at the service of 'a vast, vulgar, and meretricious beauty'

(p. 105). Moreover, Gatsby continues to believe that his wealth is the key to his regaining Daisy and their lost time. Barbour argues that since these two dreams are ultimately incompatible, Gatsby is inevitably destroyed: one cancels out the other (Barbour, 1973, p. 298ff). To put it another way, Gatsby lacks the sense of history which Carraway possesses. Carraway sees that Gatsby's dream is bound to fail because historically the American dream failed in its ideals of equality, liberty and opportunity. Thus the novel recapitulates this failure, without giving credence to or support for the dream. As Callahan puts it: 'in the pages of *Gatsby*, Fitzgerald notes the life cycle of American culture and the symptoms of its disease' (Callahan, 1972, p. 61). The American dream does not fail in the 1920s; it had failed earlier, when it became inextricably part of the materialism in American society. Gatsby's dream is similarly made up of both dreams. Carraway finds the dream attractive but knows it is bound to fail: 'Fitzgerald begins by exposing the corruption of that dream in industrial America; he ends by discovering that the pursuit is universally seductive and perpetually damned' (Fussell, 1952, p. 245).

East and West

While the approaches to the novel outlined above are deeply opposed, there are points of agreement between them. Both represent aspects of the socio–historical approach, with the assumption that *The Great Gatsby* is a novel about the condition of American society at a particular time. More specifically, both sides take for granted that the novel is somehow about the American dream; the difference arises over Fitzgerald's treatment of it. The critical debate then, can be summarized as follows. A standard view is that Fitzgerald is demonstrating the corruption of the dream in the twentieth century, particularly in the 1920s. Yet Gatsby remains heroic, because he embodies the uncorrupted elements of this dream, elements which give him a dignity lacking in the other characters. As Carraway expresses it, Gatsby was finally 'all right', as opposed to 'what preyed on Gatsby, what foul dust floated in the wake of his dreams' (p. 8). The alternative view is that Fitzgerald is critical of the American dream itself, seeing it as an illusion of liberty and openness, but which has always been historically ineffectual. It was invalidated by its crude association with materialism, and the career of Gatsby reflects historical failure. The views of Carraway on Gatsby's heroism cannot ultimately be trusted, as Carraway is a flawed narrator as well as a character easily impressed by large gestures and ambitions, of which he himself is incapable.

Since both of these approaches consider the opposition in the novel between East and West, it is worth focusing on this issue, particularly as Carraway claims it to be one of the most relevant facts to the story: 'I see now that this has been a story of the West . . . we possessed some deficiency in common which made us subtly unadaptable to Eastern life' (p. 183).

In an influential argument, Mizener claimed that the East–West contrast in the novel was primarily about value and lost values. The novel is 'a kind of tragic pastoral, with the East exemplifying urban sophistication and culture and corruption, and the Middle West . . . the simple virtues' (Mizener, 1951, pp. 175–6). This view contributes to the argument that Gatsby represents a set of values which contemporary America, epitomized by the East, has lost. In a small way, this conflict is reflected in West Egg and East Egg, since Tom and Daisy live on the fashionable Eastern side, while Nick and Gatsby are on West Egg. But as others have indicated, the issue is not so straightforward. Carraway names all of the novel's leading characters as 'Westerners', not only Gatsby. The values of the West are not all those of 'simple virtue'; Dan Cody, for instance, had brought to the East 'the savage violence of the frontier brothel and saloon' (p. 107). While Tom's extra-marital behaviour seems to be tolerated more in the East, his affair with the chambermaid was out West, in Santa Barbara (pp. 83–4).

Furthermore, as Ornstein remarks, the West evoked in the novel is scarcely appealing; it represents 'dull rectitude' and Nick escapes to it at the end of the novel, in his retreat to moral certainty (Ornstein, 1957, p. 56). Stallman points out that all the 'Westerners' cited by Nick are actually 'dishonest' (Stallman, 1961, p. 135). Also, Gatsby's tragic end is not brought about by the gangsters and the racketeers of the East. He is 'the victim of his own small-town notions of virtue and chivalry' (Ornstein, 1957, p. 59). Instead of being content to have an affair with Daisy (acceptable behaviour in the East), his sense of propriety demands marriage. More directly, his death is caused by his supposedly chivalrous protection of Daisy after the death of Myrtle Wilson.

Again, this critical disagreement points back to the different attitudes to the American dream. If the opposition between East and West were as simple as Mizener proposed, then one could accept that Fitzgerald is showing the demise of the American dream in the corrupt East. But since it is more complex, so too is Fitzgerald's notion of the dream and its historical circumstance. In fact, as with the symbols of the novel, the opposition of East and West is suggestive rather than schematic. Part of *The Great Gatsby*'s power to provoke such disagreement is part of its overall power as a work of art.

Character

Critics have tended to accept that *The Great Gatsby* is very much a novel about character conflict, and that the novel's themes are to a large degree expressed through the characters. That is, the characters could be said to have symbolic or representative roles. One of the technical advances made by Fitzgerald from his earlier novels was in using a limited number of characters. There are only five characters (Gatsby, Nick, Tom and Daisy Buchanan, Jordan Baker) who could be considered major. Myrtle Wilson and George Wilson have comparatively minor roles, and there are several more minor characters who play a significant part but who are sketched rather than characterized. These include Wolfsheim, Michaelis, the owl-eyed man, Klipspringer, and Henry Gatz. The success of *The Great Gatsby* has depended very much on the quality of Fitzgerald's characterization, and also on the use of the minor figures. In a celebrated book on the genre of the novel, E.M. Forster made a distinction between the more complex characters represented by an author, and the more accessible, 'surface' characters. He called the former 'round' characters, and the latter, 'flat', demonstrating that flat characters play an important part in the movement of the narrative (Forster, 1927, pp. 73–84).

We have seen already how the debate over Carraway's character affects the views of Gatsby and hence the themes of the entire novel. But the interaction between the novel's major characters is also crucial. The characters do not exist in isolation from each other, and, as in drama, the central themes are expressed through their conflict and interaction. Fitzgerald's chosen technique ensures that we see this interaction; that is, almost everyone has some communication or relationship with Carraway, and the impressions he forms become ours. But there is also a series of interrelationships among the leading characters. The central thematic conflict of the novel can be stated in character terms: Tom Buchanan against Gatsby. Both of course are intimate with Daisy; in simple terms, she brings them together. Gatsby and Buchanan are also related to Nick, and in some ways the novel shows Nick's losing sympathy with Tom and coming to respect and admire Gatsby. Class also links some characters: Jordan, Tom and Daisy. Although it is emphasized that he is not a man of leisure, Nick himself belongs tenuously to this class, by virtue of his manners, through having been at Yale with Tom, and because he is a distant cousin of Daisy. His relationship with Jordan springs partly from this alliance with the Buchanans; but, by the same token, when he is disillusioned and angry at the Buchanans he dissolves his relationship with her.

The Wilsons also represent significant links in the novel, for example, Tom exercises a degree of control over both Myrtle and George. The relation between Tom, Myrtle and George makes an ironic contrast with the relation between Gatsby, Daisy and Tom. Further, the relations between the Wilsons and the Buchanans are quite complex; Daisy is responsible for the death of Myrtle, while Tom is comparably responsible for the death of Gatsby, sending George Wilson to kill him.

The main point here is that while assessment of individual character is important, it can also lead to a misrepresentation of the overall work. The characters do not exist in isolation from each other, and their continual interaction is important. In fact, this use of different interacting characters was a recurring element in Fitzgerald's work, and is especially evident in his long short story, 'May Day' (1920). Further, emphasis on single characters does no justice to the novel as something written, to its symbols and motifs; nor to the effects achieved by point of view. A good example here would be when Carraway describes Tom after the accident which killed Myrtle. Carraway writes that

Tom pushed through the crowd with 'authoritative' arms (p. 148). Of course this endorses something we already know of Tom; he is a strong physical presence, and he acts decisively. But because of Fitzgerald's technique, the detail also tells us something about Carraway. Tom's authority impresses him because it is something he lacks. In spite of this danger of misrepresentation, it is useful to look at critical debate over individual characters, since interpretations have often depended on views about one particular character.

Gatsby

Among Fitzgerald's proposed titles for the novel were *Trimalchio* or *Trimalchio in West Egg*, and right up to the last minute he considered a title with the name Trimalchio in it (Fitzgerald, 1963, pp. 169, 170, 177). Although the title did not survive, a reference to this figure remains in the novel. When Gatsby's parties end, Carraway writes that his 'career as Trimalchio' was finished (p. 119). Trimalchio is a figure in *Satyricon* by Petronius, written in the first century. He is a type rather than a rounded character, representing the newly rich upstart, vulgar in his ostentatious wealth. One can speculate on why Fitzgerald dropped the name from the title; it emphasizes only one aspect of Gatsby, and thereby lessens the ambiguity that is essential to the novel. Gatsby is both Trimalchio and 'great'. Some critics have noted, however, that without Carraway's narrative which elevates the character of Gatsby, he would be merely a Trimalchio, or worse, a criminal Trimalchio: 'Gatsby is a boor, a roughneck, a fraud, a criminal. His taste is vulgar, his behavior ostentatious, his love adolescent, his business dealings ruthless and dishonest' (Scrimgeour, 1966, p. 73).

The alternative is to recognize what Carraway himself does: that in spite of his faults and vulgarity, Gatsby is great because he is dignified and ennobled by his dream. He becomes a kind of Promethean idealist. This view of Gatsby acknowledges the vulgarity of his personality, as does Carraway himself, but recognizes also the changing response that Gatsby provokes in his narrator. A standard view of Gatsby is an acceptance of Carraway's own assessment. Gatsby is 'great' because of his dream, which distinguishes him from the other, disillusioned, characters, who have lost the capacity to wonder and to dream. The weakness of this view is that it all depends on Carraway, who is far from being a disinterested observer of the action. As one critic puts it, the 'Nick story is inseparable from the Gatsby story' (Stallman, 1961, p. 136).

If we for the moment accept Carraway's narration, however, we can examine how Gatsby's dream ennobles him. Lockridge writes that Gatsby's dream has 'three basic and related parts: the desire to repeat the past, the desire for money, and the desire for incarnation of "unutterable visions" in the material earth' (Lockridge, 1968, p. 11). As noted above, these are not necessarily so distinct. For Gatsby, Daisy represents all of these dreams. Her house epitomizes the wealth and status to which the boy James Gatz aspired, his desire to repeat the past is centred on recapturing an experience with her, and she represents the 'material earth' on which his 'vision' has become focused. However, for Carraway, it is the romantic desire to defeat time which is at the heart of the dream. Of the Fitzgerald stories that are closest to *The Great Gatsby*, 'Winter Dreams' and ' "The Sensible Thing" ' are most striking in this respect. Both stories are about loss. In spite of his financial success, Dexter Green loses Judy Jones and also the dream that she had inspired. George O'Kelly, again financially successful, regains Jonquil Cary, but in doing so realizes the loss of his dreams. Gatsby refuses to accept these losses, however. He continues to believe that he can regain Daisy and can repeat the past. Instead of accepting loss stoically, he Romantically rebels against time.

In calling Gatsby's dream 'Romantic', the term is being used with more precision than usual. Fitzgerald was a great admirer of the Romantic poets, particularly of Keats. The title for *Tender is the Night* was taken from Keats's 'Ode to a Nightingale', and he called the 'Ode on a Grecian Urn', 'unbearably beautiful' (Fitzgerald, 1963, p. 88). This latter poem is of special relevance to Gatsby's dream, since, in part, it involves the relationship between love and time. Keats praises the urn because it freezes time; thus the woman on the urn 'cannot fade'. Gatsby dreams of similarly freezing time. Dexter Green and George O'Kelly had to face the fading of the beloved's beauty, or the passing of hope, and they undergo a crisis which will probably result in them accepting these losses. Gatsby defies such loss, such passing of time, and in this his Romantic heroism lies.

However, Gatsby's dream is bound to fail because its elements, as cited by Lockridge, are in conflict. His dream is an abstract idealism, but it becomes rooted in the material, rather than transcending it. Thus, he is deluded by the belief that making money will provide him with social position or help preserve youth and in becoming centred on Daisy, his belief in the capacity to transcend time will be dashed. That is, in simply being human, mortal and thereby subject to change and time, Daisy cannot fulfil Gatsby's dream. In kissing Daisy, he had 'forever wed his unutterable visions to her perishable breath' (p. 118). Because her breath is perishable, he cannot repeat the past with her.

Another significant feature of Gatsby's character is his naïvety, particularly as regards manners and politeness. (In *Satyricon*, Trimalchio's lack of the right manners was the source of much comedy.) In part, this is strongly related to the issues of class in the novel. Gatsby has acquired the wealth associated with the leisure class, but not their manners or 'breeding'. Critics usually link this aspect to the idea of the lost American dream: the supposedly open society is in fact closed, and governed by a particular class. This belief also leads Gatsby to his destruction in that he possesses a naïve sense of honour and chivalry, making him an easy prey for the more ruthless Buchanan.

Carraway also does not insist upon the criminal dealings of Gatsby; these are merely suggested to the reader. This may be because Fitzgerald himself knew too little about organized crime to be able to write convincingly about it, or it may have served his overall design of making Gatsby mysterious. In any case, telling the story from Carraway's point of view does to some extent justify the lack of detail. Not only is Carraway fairly ignorant of such activities but he has idealized Gatsby. Recognizing this, critics have often focused on Carraway's character as the key to the novel.

Nick Carraway

If one were merely to recount the events of *The Great Gatsby*, the novel could easily be made to sound trivial or melodramatic. Of course, the novel is neither and that is a tribute to Fitzgerald's art, especially his handling of symbol, character, and point of view. It is Carraway who alerts us to the dignity and depth of Gatsby's character, and suggests the relation of his tragedy to the American situation. But the character of Carraway himself is somewhat problematic. Critics have been divided into those who accept Carraway's version of himself and the events at face value, and those who have seen him as a non-authoritative narrator with an inadequate point of view.

These latter have focused particularly on the gap between Nick's account of himself as honest and careful, and his actions in the novel. The discrepancy evident between account and action has led to the judgement that he is a hypocritical self-deceiver. By far the most extreme critic of Carraway is Stallman, in an essay that has been called a 'strange tirade' (Hoffman, 1962, p. 14). Stallman notes that we cannot always accept Nick's versions of the novel's events because of his tendency to 'camouflage' the truth, to evade being specific (Stallman, 1961, p. 134). For instance, did Nick sleep with Jordan Baker? Was he engaged to the woman he left in the middle West? Nick neatly avoids being specific, he is unable emotionally to commit himself, his 'honesty' is little more than a sham, and his sense of the moral is nothing more than 'keeping up appearances' (Stallman, 1961, p. 138). Jordan comes to recognize these features of Carraway and their final conversation helps clarify them for the reader. He is after all 'a bad driver' and not very 'honest' or 'straightforward' (pp. 184–5). These characteristics would, for Stallman, make Carraway an extreme example of the inadequate narrator, much more untrustworthy than the governess in 'The Turn of the Screw' and Dowell in *The Good Soldier*.

Stallman is not alone in recognizing the importance of the final conversation between Nick and Jordan. But another interpretation of it has been proposed. Callahan argues that there has been a sexual attachment between Nick and Jordan. The issue which is understood in this conversation is whether they ought to marry. According to the code that Nick has hitherto obeyed, the honourable thing for him to do is propose to Jordan, and her comment shows her anger at his failure to do so: 'I thought you were rather an honest, straightforward person. I thought it was your secret pride'. Nick replies that he is too old to lie to himself 'and call it honour' (p. 185). He thus indicates that he believes more in personal integrity than in the code he should obey (Callahan, 1972, pp. 42–3). And yet, in the very next scene, he contradicts this, obeying the social code by shaking hands with Tom, without regard to his personal attitude to him. On the whole, Stallman's view that Nick seeks to evade emotional commitment to another seems correct.

This evasion has already been communicated to the reader; Nick says of himself that he is both 'within and without' events (p. 42). He seems to have simply ran away from the rumoured engagement 'out West' (p. 26), and even during the summer he has an affair but allows it to 'blow quietly away' (p. 63). However, he has sexual fantasies about the women in the New York streets, fantasies deriving from his 'haunting loneliness' (p. 63). The fantasies represent vicarious pleasure without lasting commitment, allowable to him on the premise that 'no one would ever know or disapprove'. Again, they represent his evasion of responsibility and emotional commitment. At the end of the novel he retreats to the safe middle West, to his comfortable 'provincial squeamishness', where he wants all decisions made for him, and 'the world to be in uniform and at a sort of moral attention forever' (pp. 186, 8). When Tom's mistress calls during the Buchanan dinner party, Nick feels like telephoning for the police, an instinct that reveals his deep need for some moral order imposed from without (p. 22). Even Nick's sense of the moral seems subordinate to a desire for neatness and correctness. When he goes to see Jordan for the last time he does so from a desire to 'leave things in order' (p. 184). When he turns down Gatsby's offer to join him in a deal, he does so not on the grounds of its immorality or illegitimacy, but because his sense of propriety is outraged (pp. 89–90).

All of this evidence counters Carraway's claim to be 'one of the few honest people' that he has known (p. 66). However, Nick cannot be utterly untrustworthy to us. As narrator, he is all we have, and if Stallman's perspective obtained, the novel would be 'chaos', which it manifestly is not (Hoffman, 1962, p. 14). If Carraway were utterly dishonest, there would be no reason to trust anything he tells us. Did Wilson murder Gatsby? Did Gatsby's father really turn up at the funeral? The mistrust of the narrator cannot be so extreme as to call the very events into question.

Critics have also speculated on the attraction that Carraway feels towards Gatsby. To some extent, this is a necessary technique on Fitzgerald's part. He introduces Gatsby last of the major characters, in a way that makes Carraway's first dislike of him very clear. Since Carraway has already guided our moral attitude towards the Buchanan set, however, from the start Gatsby seems an intriguing and attractive alternative. But more than a technical issue is involved here. Carraway comes to admire Gatsby, in part because he has grown increasingly disillusioned with the Buchanans but also because Gatsby is a kind of fantasy figure for him. The timid, self-limited, clerkly Carraway, unable emotionally to commit himself to someone, is drawn to the ambitious, idealistic, Romantic figure. Nick seems fated to sell bonds or to play a role in the family hardware business, rather than to become a racketeer. Perhaps his refusal to take up Gatsby's offer is based on timidity and on the recognition that he is fundamentally unsuited to it. But, perhaps more than anything else, Nick is attracted to Gatsby's ability to believe in something, to hope. Carraway himself is disillusioned, cynical, and somewhat pessimistic. Gatsby, however, has a freshness, optimism, and vitality which he finds appealing. This is one of the qualities he finds in Gatsby's very smile (p. 54). 'What Nick values in Gatsby are qualities he himself lacks: spontaneity; sensitivity outward; and, finally, that capacity for hope crushed in Carraway by the burden of history' (Callahan, 1972, p. 33). Accordingly, Nick is a 'foil to Gatsby'; he sees his positive qualities and emphasizes them for us (Hanzo, 1957, p. 62).

During the novel, Nick increasingly distances himself from the Buchanans, a process that can clearly be seen during the successive parties by which Fitzgerald structures the novel. Thus, one can measure Nick's acceptance of Gatsby by contrasting the first party at the Buchanan's with the last, 'broken' party with the same group and Gatsby at the Plaza Hotel. Even at the first party, though, Nick is ill at ease. He is embarrassed by Tom's talk, by his mistress telephoning, and irritated by their enquiries about his supposed engagement. But Nick continues, even at the end of the novel, to obey the proprieties he was brought up to accept.

Nick is not the central character of the novel, and he does not even properly belong to the novel's central conflict. But he is an important character, as well as the narrator, in that when we assess his character we are also assessing the validity of his perspective on the others.

Tom Buchanan

By contrast with Gatsby and Carraway, Tom seems a straight-forward character. In fact, Fitzgerald was proud of his portrayal of the vulgar, hypocritical, brutal bigot. 'I suppose he's the best character I've ever done' (Fitzgerald, 1963, p. 173). Few critics have pointed out that, like Gatsby, he too represents something of the American character. His name refers back to James Buchanan (1791–1868), the last President during slavery. This fact makes Tom's racism much more than caricature; the sentiments he expresses about the 'coloured Empires' represent dangerous bigotry (p. 19). The opposition between Gatsby and Tom can be considered as that between the man of imagination and vision, and that of the ruthlessly practical man; or even of that between soul and body, since so much emphasis is placed on Tom's physical presence. It is a character conflict that Fitzgerald used again in his novels. In *Tender is the Night*, Dick Diver's wife leaves him for Tommy Barban, whose name even suggests 'barbarian'. In *The Last Tycoon*, Fitzgerald planned to have Monroe Stahr engaged in a losing battle with Bill Brady. Buchanan, Barban and Brady are all better equipped than their opponents to live in the conditions of the modern world. They are practical and non-idealistic, but also shallow, and mistrustful of emotion. One can contrast Tom's mawkish sadness over the dog biscuits with Gatsby's emotion, for example, at the green light on the Buchanan dock (pp. 186, 27–8). As Bewley memorably puts it, Tom is 'coaxing himself to tears over a half-finished box of dog biscuits' (Bewley, 1954, p. 51). Listing these features of Tom could make him seem almost a comic caricature, but he is also 'dangerous' (Barbour, 1973, p. 290). His racist and reactionary views are not harmless. It is also important not to forget that Tom is a physically intimidating figure. Carraway considers his body 'cruel' and Daisy describes him as 'hulking' and 'a brute of a man' (pp. 13, 18). His presence often suggests his potential for violence. It seems he has badly bruised Daisy, and his violent side emerges more fully when he breaks Myrtle's nose (pp. 18, 43).

As a portrait of the wealthy man of leisure, Tom shares certain characteristics with 'The Rich Boy' Anson Hunter. Hunter breaks up an aunt's harmless friendship out of a sense of propriety, of family honour and the solidarity of the rich. Similarly, Tom's appeal to Daisy, when their relationship is threatened, is not to his supposed love for her, but to the idea that Gatsby's wealth is criminally obtained. He is the 'wrong sort' for her. The victory over Gatsby is based on the same sense of class solidarity and responsibility. Like Hunter, Fitzgerald suggests, Tom lacks emotional maturity. He will go on 'forever seeking, a little wistfully, for the dramatic turbulence of some irrecoverable football game' (p. 12). His supposedly stunted growth is implied several times by Carraway: Tom has achieved 'such an acute limited excellence at twenty-one that everything afterward savours of anticlimax' (p. 12). In some respects, Daisy and Tom are victims of a culture that values youth and its promises. Although Tom is thirty, and Daisy twenty-three, the Buchanans seem older, more middle-aged. Fitzgerald put the idea succintly in the notes for *The Last Tycoon*: 'There are no second acts in American lives' (Fitzgerald, 1941, p. 196). Youth is all, and without the promises of youth there is nothing. Part of the contrast between Tom and Gatsby is that Gatsby believes still in those promises, and in the 'orgastic future' (p. 188). The promises prove illusory for him, but, as Carraway recognizes, their very presence raises him above the one-dimensional Tom.

Daisy Buchanan

While she plays an important part in the narrative, Daisy is sometimes considered one of the few weaknesses in the novel. Fitzgerald himself was uneasy at her characterization, and felt that if the book failed commercially it would be due to there being 'no important woman character' (Fitzgerald, 1963, pp. 173, 180). However, this last comment by Fitzgerald is revealing. Rather than strengthen Daisy's character and obey the commercial demands of the market, there were clear artistic reasons for the vagueness and emptiness of Daisy's characterization. For one thing, like Tom she has an inner emptiness; in her case it is expressed through her boredom and cynicism. She is presented constantly in reaction with others. Of course, to a degree, Fitzgerald has guaranteed this by having one of the characters tell the story; as noted above, the characters are constantly in interaction. But Daisy seems afraid of being alone, as though she has no inner self which would make solitude bearable (Gatsby, by contrast, is presented as a solitary character). After Daisy's marriage, Jordan Baker tells us that she would be uneasy if Tom left for a moment (p. 83). Her intellectual limitations are stressed at several times, and the reader hardly finds her claims to sophistication very convincing (p. 24). In part, Daisy is a grown-up version of the 'flappers' that Fitzgerald had written about in his earlier work. These girls have grown up into vacant, bored, 'sophisticated' women. Fitzgerald's own delight in the flapper has been replaced by criticism; Daisy now resembles one of the bored and unfulfilled women from *The Waste Land*. 'What'll we do with ourselves this afternoon?' she asks, 'and the day after that, and the next thirty years?' (p. 124). One of the women of *The Waste Land* asks the same question 'What shall we do tomorrow? / What shall we ever do?' (Eliot, 1922, lines 133–4).

In spite of all these limitations, Daisy has the power to charm. Although from the start Carraway does not altogether trust her, he is careful to present her attractive qualities. In particular, her voice is emphasized, and even described as a 'deathless song' (p. 103). This odd phrase makes a link between Daisy and Keats's nightingale. In fact, Fitzgerald went to some lengths to have a mention of a nightingale; at the Buchanan dinner party, Daisy fancies she hears one singing (p. 22). Since the bird is not a native of America, its presence is jokingly attributed to its having come over on a liner (p. 22). Although this technique is clumsy, it draws attention to Daisy's function in the novel, that is, Gatsby's dream becomes centred upon her. Carraway emphasizes that she is unworthy of it. The critic Brian Way expresses the issue well: 'The core of Gatsby's tragedy is not only that he lived by dreams, but that the woman and the class and the way of life . . . fell so far short [of them] . . . Daisy is a trivial, callous, cowardly woman' (Way, 1980, p. 109).

It is also true that Daisy actually represents material wealth to Gatsby. Again, the connection of wealth with physical attractiveness was common in Fitzgerald's work. His notebooks include this description of a young woman: 'She was lovely and expensive, and about nineteen' (Fitzgerald, 1956, p. 133). Gatsby describes Daisy's voice as 'full of money' (p. 126). Again, this association in Daisy herself points to the weakness of Gatsby's dream. It is involved at once with the romantic and the material, in a way that inevitably means its destruction. As one critic puts it, the theme of *The Great Gatsby* is 'the potential tragedy of passionately idealizing an unworthy and even sinister object' (Miller, 1967, p. 121). Daisy is the 'object'.

The 'money' in Daisy's voice suggests also the exclusive club of the wealthy to which she and Tom belong. To Nick, this closeness between them is at first a mystery. Even though, at their dinner party, she is angry with Tom and treats him coldly, she looks at Nick 'as if she had asserted her membership in a rather distinguished secret society to which she and Tom belonged' (p. 24). The gesture is repeated at the end of the evening when the Buchanans accompany Nick to the door. When they patch up their marriage at the novel's end, the gestures of conspiracy are repeated over their untouched supper (p. 152). This is the basis of the critical view of Daisy's 'cowardice'; at the moment of crisis she rejects Gatsby and 'retreats' with Tom into the safety of their money. They are 'careless people': 'they smashed up things and creatures and then retreated back into their money or their vast carelessness, or whatever it was that kept them together, and let other people clean up the mess they had made' (p. 186).

Jordan Baker

While critics have hardly seen the need to debate the character of Jordan, they have focused on her significance in the narrative structure of *The Great Gatsby*. Technically, she is a *ficelle*: a thread necessary to the pattern of the narrative, providing accounts of events that Carraway could not otherwise have known. She informs Nick of Daisy's wartime meeting with Gatsby, and of her subsequent marriage to Tom. It is indirectly because of her that Carraway becomes involved with Gatsby's affairs. Furthermore, her presence in the novel is important for the light it throws on the character of Carraway. She highlights his weaknesses, and if she is a 'bad driver' then so is he (pp. 184–5). She exposes him for not being the honest, careful man he prefers to consider himself.

Nick is impressed by her celebrity status, and he also tries to 'ingratiate' himself with her aunt (pp. 64, 108).

In character terms, critics often relate Jordan to Daisy, in that both are seen as 'careless' and 'dishonest' (Way, 1980, p. 118). Nick kisses Jordan after hearing her tell the story of Gatsby and Daisy, an act that makes their relationship seem a parallel to the larger passion (pp. 86–7). Nick tells us that she is 'incurably dishonest' and critics have taken this assessment at face value (p. 64). In fact, when one considers the scarcity of concrete information about Jordan (except that supplied by her ex-lover), it is surprising how readily she has been impugned. 'Cynicism' and 'irresponsibility' are terms usually applied to her. One critic calls her 'a professional tennis [sic] player who has succumbed to the ennui of the frantic search for novelty and excitement to which she and others of her post-war generation had devoted themselves' (Hanzo, 1957, p. 64). Lionel Trilling calls her 'vaguely homosexual' (Trilling, 1950, p. 111), while another critic rather solemnly informs us that 'Sterility characterizes the soulless Jordan' (Stallman, 1961, p. 138).

While Jordan is not particularly an ambiguous or 'rounded' character, it is interesting that critics should be so prepared to offer such extreme moral judgements of her, and the reader might well be surprised to discover how immoral she is. After all, if she is to be condemned for her lies, and for having slept with Nick, then Carraway is equally immoral. He is hypocritical too, as Jordan points out; he feigns honesty and straightforwardness.

Part Two: Appraisal

Introduction

My own critical attitude is based on the recognition that the literary work has a public existence, though that is not the only existence it has. My instinct is to agree with Matthew Arnold when he wrote that art is 'a criticism of life' and to say, more specifically, that a novel is an examination of society. It need not be a 'criticism' of society: some novels endorse existing social systems and relations, and to some degree the very form of the novel is conservative. Its closed form provides a kind of comforting assurance to readers that the world is manageable and knowable; the novel itself developed as a genre during the rise of the middle classes. In fact, the current post-modernist concern with the lack of closure in the novel is in part due to this realization. The contemporary novel may actually frustrate, disconcert and discomfort the reader in ways that make it no longer a bourgeois text to be consumed and to provide comfort.

A further point that needs to be made is that social systems tend to institutionalize dissent, and by so doing reduce its power, its capacity to disturb. Art works which are disturbingly rebellious in one generation are often, by a variety of processes, made tame in the next. *The Great Gatsby* itself is a case in point. I would argue that *The Great Gatsby* is a powerful criticism of American society, as damning a document as *The Waste Land*. But to a large degree Fitzgerald's criticism has been deflected by the very processes of that society. For example, filmed versions of *The Great Gatsby* have tended to suggest that the book is not a criticism of society at all, but a book of romantic nostalgia, or a book about the Jazz Age, therefore demanding an air of opulence. The novel itself has become a vehicle for all kinds of commercial purposes, such as the selling of clothes, cooking utensils and drinks (see Anderson, 1985, p. 23). One often comes across public houses or wine bars named after Gatsby, in vague and quite undiscriminating attempts to borrow some supposed sense of dignified wealth. Readers of the novel can perceive the irony here.

However, these are not the only ways in which a literary text's power to disturb can be dissipated. Some would argue that putting *The Great Gatsby* on syllabi in schools, colleges and universities is another way of diverting its impact, another way of institutionalizing dissent. The power of literature, this argument goes, thereby becomes safely contained in the classroom, in lecture notes and examination questions, rather than becoming a force in the whole lives of people. There is much to be said for this argument, particularly if the process of making *The Great Gatsby* into a 'set text' is accompanied by a teaching approach which considers it primarily as a structure of words. In theory at least, a formalist approach to this novel could become so extreme that the reader might forget that it deals with people, with a society and with living issues.

Criticism itself can become concerned with a series of apparently trivial issues, and the more trivial the issue, then the more our attention is being drawn away from the text's power. However, issues which may seem minor often increase our appreciation of the novel. What colour is Daisy's hair? By which of Gatsby's cars is Myrtle killed? On the night Myrtle is killed, from where does Gatsby telephone for the taxi which takes him home to West Egg? Although they sound fairly trivial, these questions can indicate some important facts about the novel. Fitzgerald's confusion over Daisy's hair suggests his attitude to women in the novel; they are poorly realized and always secondary to the male characters. The refusal to be specific about the car which kills Myrtle must be seen as deliberate, but is the vagueness about Gatsby's taxi a slip on Fitzgerald's part?

In approaching *The Great Gatsby* as a 'criticism of life' criticism itself has a responsibility to help us appreciate the novel, and whatever critical method we adopt, we should never lose sight of the social and public existence of the work. In this part of the book, I shall examine several aspects of *The Great Gatsby* which seem to me to have been somewhat neglected, or in which a contemporary reader might be most interested.

The Clock and the Moon

In *The Great Gatsby*, time is of crucial importance. The word itself, and other words related to it, recur frequently. Time is important thematically, being related to Gatsby's dream, which is deeply concerned with the desire to escape or defeat time, to 'repeat the past'. This aspect of his dream is comparable to one of the ideas inherent in English Romanticism. Coleridge temporarily escaped from time's domination when he had the vision which led to his writing 'Kubla Khan' (1797). The odes of Keats which Fitzgerald so admired also include the longing to escape from time; to soar above it like the nightingale, or to be removed from it like the Grecian urn. The urn, in particular, is praised and celebrated because it has achieved timelessness. Gatsby's 'mythic' status suggests that he too is timeless.

But the experience of closely reading *The Great Gatsby* makes us realize how deeply it is concerned with time's passing, with the anti-Romantic view of time. Indeed, mention of Gatsby's dream is often textually contrasted with some symbol suggesting time. One of the best examples of this occurs in Chapter 6, as Carraway imagines the dreams of the young Jimmy Gatz taking shape:

> The most grotesque and fantastic conceits haunted him in his bed at night. A universe of ineffable gaudiness spun itself out in his brain while the clock ticked on the washstand and the moon soaked with wet light his tangled clothes upon the floor. (p. 105).

In part this is Rudolph Miller from 'Absolution' in the process of inventing Blatchford Sarnemington. But it is more than that, and close examination of the passage should reveal something of the power of Fitzgerald's style. Two opposing symbols are used: the clock and the moon. The clock of course is time, representing all that Gatsby needs to defeat. The moon represents Romantic possibility. Things seen in moonlight become unfamiliar, strange, and invested with the possibilities of the imagination. We first see Gatsby in the moonlight, paying homage to the green dock light (pp. 27–8), and at the novel's end, the rising moon is appropriate to Carraway's thoughts of Gatsby. The moon suggests also Gatsby's parties, where it was produced as if from a caterer's basket (p. 49). The phrase 'ineffable gaudiness' hints at the extravagant colours of Gatsby's clothes, his parties and cars; in fact, his whole 'career as Trimalchio'. The 'tangled clothes' on the floor remind us of the pile of shirts he shows to Daisy (p. 99).

In a sense, the ambitions and defeat of Gatsby are concentrated here, in a passage closely linked to symbols and incidents that recur in the novel. Gatsby's dreams were born under the moonlight in childhood, but accompanying them even then was the ticking of the clock, and Gatsby will never escape that ticking. Furthermore, the moonlight has 'soaked' the clothes, suggesting how far Gatsby's failure lay in an inability to keep the material separate from the purity of the imagination. As suggested earlier in this book, Gatsby's tragedy was that his dreams became focused on the unworthy, mortal Daisy. When he is reunited with her in Carraway's house, the clock is once more present, in a way that seems almost comic. Gatsby almost breaks an old clock of Carraway's, but, significantly, it survives intact. Symbolically, Fitzgerald suggests how even at the moment Gatsby's dream is moving to fulfilment, time will not be stopped. The incident anticipates the failure of Gatsby to regain Daisy.

From evidence such as this, one could argue that one of the prominent themes of *The Great Gatsby* is the inevitability of escaping time. The Romantically inspired Gatsby attempts to, but fails abjectly. W.H. Auden's poem, 'As I walked out one evening' (1937), expresses the same idea; time is our final reality, destroying both ideal and illusion. In Auden's poem, the lover who claims his love will last for ever receives a reply:

> But all the clocks in the city
> Began to whirr and chime:
> 'O let not Time deceive you,
> You cannot conquer Time.
>
> 'In the burrows of the Nightmare
> Where Justice naked is,
> Time watches from the shadow
> And coughs when you would kiss.
>
> (Auden, 1937)

In the novel, Nick possesses this knowledge, but Gatsby does not. This makes Gatsby's failure all the more poignant for Nick. He imagines that after the dream is defeated, Gatsby sees nature itself differently, without any Romantic sense of it being mystical and benign: 'He must have looked up at an unfamiliar sky through frightening leaves and shivered as he found what a grotesque thing a rose is and how raw the sunlight was upon the scarcely created grass' (p. 168).

The world for him now is 'material without being real' (p. 168); it was real when it was invested with his dream; now it is merely 'material' and points towards death. The leaves are 'frightening' because they are changing colour, thereby reflecting the mutability of nature from which we as humans are not exempt. Gatsby, Nick implies, is forced now to accept the inevitability of time and death, to accept that, as Myrtle Wilson puts it, 'You can't live forever' (p. 42). Now that he is forced to accept time, everything points to the meaninglessness of his life and his inevitable death:

> The glacier knocks in the cupboard,
> The desert sighs in the bed,
> And the crack in the tea-cup opens
> A lane to the land of the dead.
>
> (Auden, 1937)

Auden's poem is about not being deceived by illusion, and one could argue that this is a theme also in *The Great Gatsby*. Instead of being somehow an endorsement of romantic vision, the novel is actually an attack on it as illusion. Gatsby is deceived by the illusion, and it destroys him. Carraway's narrative makes this clear, since it points to our human inability to evade the relentless passing of time and the recurring clocks.

However, this conclusion can be made only if we ignore the subtleties of Fitzgerald's narrative technique for, once more, we are back to the issue of Carraway's relation to Gatsby. It can be argued that the contrast between them includes an attitude to time, and that it is Carraway rather than Gatsby who is haunted by it. There is much evidence to support this view. For example, in telling the story, Nick rarely gives us specific dates. But he suggests the dates sufficiently for us to build up a picture of the summer from June to September. We know, for instance, that the Buchanan party described in Chapter 1 takes place in the first week of June, because Daisy refers to the longest day being in two weeks' time (p. 18). The death of Myrtle and the climax of the novel come in early September, the end of summer (pp. 120, 173), and Nick leaves the East 'late in October' (p. 185). Time passes imperceptibly but relentlessly in Nick's narrative. Furthermore, Nick is often specific about the time, as though he is always looking at his watch or clock. Significantly, when he is drunk (for only the second occasion in his life), he loses a sense of time (though he still looks at his watch); 'It was nine o'clock — almost immediately afterward I looked at my watch and found it was ten' (p. 43).

It is Nick who is obsessed by the passing of time. He is the post-war cynic who would long to believe that time can be defeated, but cannot do so. If Gatsby's dream and hence Gatsby himself are characterized by the moon, then Carraway's symbol is the clock. He needs regularity in his life, a need evident in various ways. After the events of the summer, he wants the world 'in uniform' and 'at a sort of moral attention forever' (p. 8). Regularity is his defence against chaos, against nihilism. The account he gives of his schedule as a bond dealer further increases our sense that he takes refuge in work and its regular, scheduled, 'conscientious' hours (see pp. 62–4).

I have already mentioned Joseph Conrad's *Heart of Darkness* (1902) as a model for *The Great Gatsby*, in terms of the narrative point of view. In Conrad's novel, Marlow, the narrator, finds refuge in work when he cannot cope with the moral nihilism displayed by Kurtz. Work prevents Marlow from brooding on the essential 'hollowness' of life and civilization, but Kurtz does not have this defence, and is destroyed by his knowledge. While the situation in *The Great Gatsby* is not entirely similar, Carraway does, like Marlow, believe in work and regularity as ways of avoiding a sense of life's emptiness. On the day after Myrtle's death, he insists on going to work, even though his ostensible reasons are unclear (p. 160ff). In going to the office, he attempts to escape the chaotic feeling that the series of events has induced in him; however, he leaves Gatsby to face death alone. At the novel's end, he returns to the moral certainties and provincial narrowness of his middle West, another way of avoiding the unwelcome thoughts that the East has produced in him.

One of the reasons for Carraway's sense of inner emptiness is not difficult to find. In fact, it is striking that few critics have mentioned the fact that both Carraway and Gatsby are war survivors. At the end of *This Side of Paradise*, Amory Blaine considers the people of the post-war generation. They have grown up and found that all gods are dead, 'all wars fought, all faiths in man shaken' (Fitzgerald, 1920, p. 253). Since Carraway embodies this nihilism, he is inevitably attracted to Gatsby who has maintained his hope and faith. Carraway, symbolized by the clock and the watch, longs to believe with Gatsby in the promise of the moon. This view leads to an alternative perspective on the scene when Gatsby almost breaks Carraway's clock. While pointing to Gatsby's inability to defeat time, it is significant that the clock actually belongs to Carraway. The attraction to Gatsby's dream cannot overcome Nick's own dependence on time. While the scene prefigures the failure of Gatsby's reunion with Daisy, it points also to Carraway's continuing commitment to time and regularity, and his return to the mid-West.

To some degree, Nick's recognition of the inevitability of time is also evident in the very making of his narrative. For instance, as we have seen, his list of the people who came to Gatsby's parties (pp. 67–9) has several functions. It can be seen as an echo of the epic device, thereby suggesting the power of the myth of Gatsby; it can be seen as mock epic, or it can be considered a comment on the violence and restlessness characteristic of modern America. But it also grows out of a desire to preserve, based on the recognition that time will otherwise erase the names. Significantly, the list is written on a timetable, and precisely dated; both are characteristic of Nick and his inescapable sense of time and date. The list attempts to preserve and thereby give a kind of immortality to Gatsby's guests, and, in a larger way, his very narrative is intended to commemorate Gatsby's dream. Curiously, the act of preserving connects Nick to Gatsby's father. Mr Gatz shows Nick his son's schedule that he has saved for sixteen years (p. 180). Nick and Gatsby's father obey time. Recognizing that it cannot be defeated, they preserve what would otherwise be forgotten. Gatsby, the romantic, attempts to disobey time.

It is worth reiterating the point already made by other critics; that the character differences between Carraway and Gatsby are crucial to the novel. Being committed to the clock, to the 'conscientious hour' (p. 63), and wary of emotional expression and commitment, Carraway is exactly the character to be impressed by Gatsby, once his initial reservations have been overcome. He becomes both the chronicler and the defender of Gatsby; he defends Gatsby against Tom, and erases the obscenity chalked on Gatsby's step (p. 187). He even vicariously partakes of the intensity of Gatsby's emotion, as though recognizing that he cannot hope to reproduce such intensity. We see this most clearly when, moved by Jordan's telling him the story of Daisy and Gatsby, he kisses her (pp. 86–7).

In considering the conflict in the novel between the romantic and the anti-romantic, realist, attitudes in *The Great Gatsby*, symbolized respectively by the moon and the clock, it is important to realize that they are somewhat complementary. This is one of the finest achievements of the novel, and, to some extent, provides an answer to one of the critical debates the novel has stimulated. That is, whether Fitzgerald endorses the romantic vision or derides it.

As we have seen, there is clear evidence for both views. Gatsby is made ridiculous and destroyed by his illusions; Carraway also sees him as better than all of the other characters. Fitzgerald provides a complex fusion of the romantic and the cynical realist. It is worth remembering that the division between Gatsby and Carraway was a division in Fitzgerald himself: between the lover of Keats and the admirer of Eliot, the man who reputedly knew both 'Ode to a Nightingale' and *The Waste Land* by heart. Both Keats and Eliot are in *The Great Gatsby*, and the novel's overall theme emerges as the fusion between them. While Gatsby's dreams do turn out to be illusions, they are better than no illusions at all. While planning *The Great Gatsby*, Fitzgerald wrote that the 'burden' of the novel would be 'the loss of those illusions that give such color to the world so that you don't care whether things are true or false as long as they partake of the magical glory' (Mizener, 1951, p. 177). Nick comes to recognize this: with nothing to believe in, our lives are pointless, hopeless, and scarcely bearable. Even a dream that turns illusory is better than nothing. To state the theme of the novel thus is to endorse its greatness as a modern text. Both

Eugene O'Neill's *The Iceman Cometh* (1946) and Samuel Beckett's *Waiting for Godot* (1952), address the same theme: our hopes and dreams may destroy us in the end, but without them our lives are meaningless and absurd.

A Man's Book: *The Great Gatsby* and Women

Although Fitzgerald was convinced that *The Great Gatsby* was a masterpiece, and his finest work to date, he worried that its sales would be hurt by the lack of an 'important woman character' (Fitzgerald, 1963, p. 180). The narrator and the other main characters, Gatsby and Tom Buchanan, are, of course, men, and the women are defined and characterized primarily in relation to the men. As Fitzgerald himself put it, the women are 'emotionally passive' and the novel is '*a man's book*' (Fitzgerald, 1963, pp. 488, 173). Because of the strong growth of feminist criticism over the past two decades, it is interesting to re-examine these issues, and to determine the part they play in an overall assessment of the novel.

One can readily acknowledge that in general the women characters are quite secondary to the males. In particular, Daisy seems poorly realized as a character. Susan Korenman points out that Fitzgerald is unsure of the colour of her hair, describing it 'in contradictory ways' (Korenman, 1975, p. 574). When she is with her daughter, who has 'yellowy' hair, Daisy's hair is described as the same colour (*The Great Gatsby*, pp. 122-3). However, her hair is also described as 'dark' (p. 156), and is compared to 'a dash of blue paint' (p. 92). Tom, who is blond, only hesitantly includes her with Nick and the blonde Jordan Baker as 'nordic' (p. 20). Korenman interestingly suggests that most readers, though, think of Daisy's hair as blonde, mainly because Fitzgerald associates her so strongly with gold and wealth (Korenman, 1975, p. 576). The point here is not only that Fitzgerald sketched Daisy lightly, but also that her actual role in the novel is somewhat ambiguous. Hair is traditionally a symbol for fertility, and in literature a division between dark-haired and fair-haired women is often maintained, particularly in the nineteenth-century novel. The fair-haired woman is considered desirable, aloof, idealized; the dark-haired is considered sexually active and therefore more 'available'.

Fitzgerald's vagueness about Daisy reflects his confusion about her role. She is the idealized woman of Gatsby's dream. She is also the physical woman who slept with Gatsby when she was eighteen, and whose later behaviour causes his servants to gossip (pp. 155, 120). In having her fulfil both roles, Fitzgerald simply confused her hair colour.

The very idealization of Daisy may be problematic for contemporary readers of the novel. While agreeing that she is 'emotionally passive' we might feel uneasy about the unacknowledged sense in which she is a victim of Gatsby's obsession. Critics have generally seen that Gatsby's dream fails partly because it is centred on someone who proves unworthy of it. But this might not be a satisfactory way of analysing the situation. Hypothetically, the events of the novel could be retold from a feminist point of view, perhaps being narrated by Daisy herself. Clearly, a quite different novel would emerge; perhaps we would be able to see that Daisy is victimized and dehumanized by an obsessive man with whom she once slept. Since Daisy's point of view is nowhere acknowledged by Fitzgerald, we know that this is a misreading of the actual novel he wrote, but it is interesting to speculate on the thematic implications arising from the novel's representation of a masculine world view.

The very choice of Carraway as narrator increases our sense of the secondary role played by the women. Contemporary readers might quickly notice that Nick has a low opinion of women in general. This attitude could be attributed to his broadly cynical, embittered view of life, but it seems more specific than that. He seems instinctively suspicious of attractive or charming women, feeling that they use their charms for some unfair advantage. Even when professing his dislike of Daisy, he acknowledges her charm. His relation with Jordan is, naturally, more revealing. His comments about her make prominent his underlying contempt for women. For example, when considering her lies, he pompously proclaims that 'Dishonesty in a woman is a thing you never blame deeply' (p. 65). In other words, because women are generally dishonest, no moral blame can be attached to an individual woman's dishonest act. Such a belief reveals a deep-seated hatred of women. Since Nick's sexual fantasies feature anonymity, brevity, and a lack of moral or emotional commitment (p. 63), our sense of him as a misogynist increases.

That is, he will take women for sexual gratification, but without any attempt to accept them as individual human beings.

In fact, there are some hints in the narrative that Nick is a repressed homosexual. The strongest detail he recalls of his lover in the mid-West is her 'moustache of perspiration' (p. 65), and Jordan's mannish qualities are evident at several points. Again, in evaluating the narrative methods of *The Great Gatsby*, Nick's attitudes to women cannot readily be ignored. Curiously, though, Myrtle Wilson emerges as an almost tragic character. At first her pretensions to what she considers a higher class are satirized. After changing her dress in the New York apartment, her vitality gives way to 'impressive *hauteur*' (p.36), and she unconsciously apes the complaints the upper classes supposedly make about servants: 'These people! You have to keep after them all the time' (p. 38). But the reader gradually perceives that her character forms a contrast with that of Gatsby. 'You can't live forever' is a realistic recognition that time will destroy us. She does not have Gatsby's illusions concerning time, and Carraway repeatedly emphasizes her vitality, her blood.

While this is still defining the women characters in terms of their relation to men, it is worth remembering that much of Fitzgerald's technique in the novel is based upon the conflicts and interactions of all the characters. We never see Gatsby without the intervening intelligence of Carraway, and the novel's themes emerge through the conflict between Gatsby and Tom Buchanan. Further, Fitzgerald had acknowledged the market loss that his depiction of the women could produce, but he believed that such depiction was integral to the artistic purpose of the novel.

The Great Gatsby and Social Class

Fitzgerald has scarcely been analysed as a serious social critic. In some ways, the reasons for this are obvious. His social circle in the 1920s and his background of wealth seem to have disqualified Fitzgerald from being considered in the same category as writers such as Jack London, Upton Sinclair and John Steinbeck. These were writers whose socialist commitment was matched by a range of experiences demonstrating their closeness to labouring people. Steinbeck, for example, is often associated with the Depression, with Oklahoma, or with the fruit groves, canning factories and casual labour of California. Fitzgerald (who considered Steinbeck a 'phoney'), is usually associated with cosmopolitan glitter, and almost always characterized as a writer obsessed with glamour (Fitzgerald, 1963, p. 581). One of the most widely known anecdotes about Fitzgerald and Hemingway is centred on two short stories, Fitzgerald's 'The Rich Boy', and Hemingway's 'The Snows of Kilimanjaro' (1936). Introducing Anson Hunter, Fitzgerald's narrator writes that the rich 'are different from you and me' (Fitzgerald, 1987, p. 110). In 'The Snows of Kilimanjaro', an anonymous character provides a reply: 'Yes, they have more money' (Hemingway, 1961, p. 23). Hemingway's slight prompted a reply from Fitzgerald. (It should be noted that in the original magazine version of the story, Fitzgerald was actually named; in the book version, the name 'Julian' is substituted.) Fitzgerald, hurt at this characterization, pointed out the misunderstanding evident in Hemingway's view: 'Riches have *never* fascinated me, unless combined with the greatest charm or distinction' (Fitzgerald, 1963, p. 311).

In fact, Fitzgerald was not over-reacting here. In much of his writing there is a criticism of the wealthy. At times, this criticism is submerged, but it is fairly consistent. In the three short stories which are closest to *The Great Gatsby*, Fitzgerald examines the way that wealth corrupts, or the way that the wealthy form a kind of club. In 'The Rich Boy', Anson Hunter's wealth and background make him emotionally sterile and childish. In 'The Diamond as Big as the Ritz', Braddock Washington attempts to create a world insulated from history and humanity in order to protect his wealth. In part, it is obvious that Fitzgerald's criticism of the wealthy was due to his feeling that he was outside of their circle. Such a feeling forms the main theme of both 'Winter Dreams' and '"The Sensible Thing"'; it also appears in his essay 'The Crack-Up' (1936). Considering his engagement to Zelda which was broken off because of his lack of money, and restored when he made some, Fitzgerald wrote: 'The man with the jingle of money in his pocket who married the girl a year later would always cherish an abiding distrust, an animosity, towards the leisure class' (Fitzgerald, 1974, p. 47). He also writes that this hatred was not that of the revolutionary, but the 'smouldering hatred of the peasant' (p. 47).

Although Fitzgerald was writing this essay at a time of great personal strain (brought on partly by debt), the attitude is consistent with the depiction of the wealthy in the short stories and in *The Great Gatsby*. He may well have been obsessed with glamour; but he was equally concerned with failure. *The Great Gatsby* is about Gatsby's failure, not about his success. His failure to regain Daisy is completely bound up with his failure to possess a background relevant to her class. In *Tender is the Night*, Dick Diver fails because he allows himself to be led away from the demands of a profession to a life of indolence and leisure. A sense of failure is often powerful in Fitzgerald's work. In the late 1930s, he wrote seventeen stories about a character called Pat Hobby. Hobby was once a well paid screenwriter; now he is a shiftless drinker hanging around the edges of Hollywood taking whatever hack jobs come his way. There is a certain charm to these critically under-rated stories, and to the character of Hobby, but it is not the charm exerted by the wealthy characters of Fitzgerald's earlier works.

If Fitzgerald came to hate the wealthy 'with the smouldering hatred of the peasant' rather than the revolutionary's hatred, this was not always the case. The socialist writer H. G. Wells was an early influence on Fitzgerald, and at the end of *This Side of Paradise*, Amory Blaine preaches his own version of the socialist message. The long and ambitious short story 'May Day' (1920) is concerned with the interaction between different strata of society, including a group of socialist agitators. The story is about a society deeply divided by wealth and privilege, and accordingly in crisis; the title indicates both the day celebrating socialism and the 'May Day' distress call. Fitzgerald was familiar with the works of Marx, and in the 1930s he followed the intellectual path beaten by friends like Edmund Wilson, and considered himself a communist (Sklar, 1967, p. 305). Among the plans for *Tender is the Night* was one in which Dick Diver's son was to be educated in the Soviet Union, a move representing commitment to the future (Way, 1980, p. 145).

Recognition of Fitzgerald as a socially concerned writer has undoubtedly been hampered by the type of popularity his novels have enjoyed since his death, and it is worth have considering the basis of *The Great Gatsby*'s popularity. When Fitzgerald died in 1940, the novel was out of print, but it was gradually rediscovered by the reading public and eventually achieved the high critical regard it possesses today. For readers of the 1940s and later, the novel told of a past glamour, a kind of supposed age of enjoyment about which readers could be imaginatively nostalgic. As I have mentioned earlier, the notion of glamour still attaches to Gatsby, even though he is consistently presented as vulgar and ostentatious. The supposed sense of glamour has often distracted readers from the real issues of the novel. Bluntly, Fitzgerald's material, the class about which he wrote, was not that of a 1930s socialist writer such as Steinbeck. He acknowledged this in his 'Introduction' to the 1934 edition of *The Great Gatsby*: 'But, my God! it was my material, and it was all I had to deal with' (Fitzgerald, 1934, p. 109).

Given these contexts, *The Great Gatsby* is certainly a novel about the rich, but not a novel praising their charm and glamour. It is about how the wealthy preserve and maintain their social status, closing their circle against outsiders and interlopers. Fitzgerald's background gave him the chance to observe the wealthy at first hand, and several critics have pointed out how convincing his wealthy characters are. Fitzgerald understood the rich, and saw that they maintained power and prestige partly through creating an idea of 'breeding' and manners in order to exclude others from their circle. In his stimulating book on Fitzgerald, Brian Way reminds us that in the socialist novel of the 1930s the rich are stereotyped:

> Fitzgerald does not make the mistake of imagining that because the rich are corrupt, they must necessarily be weak. That fallacy was to be a part of the sentimentality of the 1930s — as we see in *The Grapes of Wrath*, where the rich appear as impotent scared little men hiding behind barbed wire and hired guns. (Way, 1980, pp. 102–3).

One of the most interesting scenes in *The Great Gatsby* occurs in Chapter 6 (pp. 108–11). One Sunday afternoon, Nick is at Gatsby's house when Tom Buchanan, a Mr Sloane, and an unnamed woman (evidently Sloane's mistress), turn up unexpectedly. Tom does not remember Gatsby from their previous meeting, but, in order to be polite, pretends that he does. Sloane's reluctance to be there and his eagerness to get away are obvious to Nick; he refuses any refreshment and sits silently. The woman, however, becomes slightly drunk and invites Gatsby and Nick to dinner. The well-bred men see the invitation for what it is, an invitation stimulated by the drinks, and therefore one to which polite decline is the correct response. Nick accordingly refuses politely. But Gatsby takes the invitation at face value, accepts it and goes to collect his coat. Meanwhile, the visitors hurriedly depart, with Sloane clearly having remonstrated with the woman. The point of the scene is that those who have inherited their wealth communicate in a series of codes which exclude others. The rich are different; and not merely because they have more money. Tom's incredulity at Gatsby's behaviour is comic, but it also indicates the seriousness of the book's themes. 'Doesn't he know she doesn't want him?' he asks, and Nick matter of factly replies, 'She says she does want him' (p. 110). Nick, as usual, is both 'within and without'; he obeys the codes but also sees that they are inherently false.

While comedy arising from class differences in manners is firmly established in European literature, the fact that such a 'comedy of manners' could exist in the United States was, Fitzgerald perceived, an indictment of his society. Having been founded as an ideally open society, in which advancement and opportunity were available to all, class differences as exhibited in manners indicate that the ideal is lost. The wealthy in *The Great Gatsby* form a kind of aristocracy, where inherited wealth is valued more than achieved wealth. Sociologists have often remarked on the aping of the European aristocracy among the wealthy in America, to the degree that even pseudo-titles, such as 'John D. Rockefeller IV' are bestowed on heirs. In a classic study called *The Rich and the Super Rich*, Ferdinand Lundberg relates the following anecdote:

> Mrs David Lion Gardiner, dowager empress of New York's proud Gardiner family, was informed that her young grandson was about to go out and play with the Rockefeller children. Mrs Gardiner forbade it. 'No Gardiner will ever play,' she said, 'with the grandchild of a gangster.' (Lundberg, 1968, p. 285).

One can immediately see the relevance of these ideas to the themes of *The Great Gatsby*. Even Nick's family, though their wealth comes from the hardware business, are proud of the rumour that they are descended from the Dukes of Buccleuch (pp. 8–9). As mentioned earlier, Tom's successful appeal to Daisy relies on her knowledge that they belong to the same class, a class superior to that of the gangster Gatsby.

While *The Great Gatsby* is deeply concerned with examining the behaviour of the wealthy, Fitzgerald, as Hemingway knew, is also aware of the charm they exert. But even this charm is seen to be illusion, attractive only to those outside the circle of the wealthy. Again, the significance of Carraway's narration must again be emphasized. Nick knows that the rich have no special charm; although he obeys their conventions and their manners, he is sufficiently an outsider to be cynical about them. Accordingly, he can see that Gatsby has been charmed by some set of illusions about the power of money, in particular by the belief that it can imprison and preserve youth and mystery (p. 155). The Buchanans themselves have no such illusion about their wealth. They are both entirely practical people; Daisy's original choice of Tom over Gatsby is based on her 'unquestionable practicality' (p. 157). That is, she simply cannot wait for Gatsby to return. Bluntly, she knows that if she waits, time will start to erode her youthful attractiveness and her value in the market for an eligible husband. The Buchanans are unsentimental about their wealth and their youth and, unlike Gatsby, they are realistic about time. They are also somehow in control of it; the sundials on their lawn suggest a realistic and non-rebellious approach to its passing (p. 12). Thus, the glamour of the rich is illusory, and their methods of preserving their status are an affront to the values on which the United States was founded. These are large and complex indictments of the class system in twentieth-century America.

In his examination of the class system, though, Fitzgerald does not confine himself to the wealthy. In some ways, he is equating the history of America with the protection of wealth. In 'The Diamond as Big as the Ritz' he wrote a parable of America's history, suggesting that the need to preserve wealth for a few was the impetus behind both the American revolution and the institution of slavery. Both are referred to in the story. The mountain's current owner is a descendant of George Washington, and his continuing ownership is made possible by the maintenance of slaves. *The Great Gatsby* also examines the history of America, from the arrival of the first settlers to the present. Fitzgerald also satirizes the ideals of success in American society. In *The Great Gatsby* the American ideals of success and social mobility are largely illusions, and, furthermore, are illusions fostered by those with an interest in maintaining the prevailing class system.

While this theme is perhaps most apparent in the way that the wealthy preserve their status, it is also evident in other ways. In 'Absolution', the discarded prologue to *The Great Gatsby*, Fitzgerald mentions that Rudolph Miller has a set of Horatio Alger books (Fitzgerald, 1987, p. 404). Since Alger is of great importance to Fitzgerald, it is worth examining the treatment of the Alger ideals in *The Great Gatsby*. Horatio Alger (1834–1899) has probably been the most widely read of all American authors; he wrote well over one hundred novels and is estimated to have sold approximately twenty million copies of them. His novels tend to follow the same pattern; a boy works his way up from poverty to respectability through hard work, thrift, and good luck. In *Ragged Dick* (1868), for example, Dick Hunter starts out as a Manhattan bootblack, sleeping on the street. By a variety of circumstances he achieves a respectable position in an office, having achieved a measure of education and some savings. In an unsophisticated way, then, the novel endorses the values of hard work, enterprise and honesty. As mentioned earlier, the novels were extremely popular among children.

It is obvious, though, that Fitzgerald perceived the larger effects of the novels. As they emphasize personal virtues, they also help to maintain the existing class system. In spite of his advancement to the position of clerk, Dick comes to no understanding of an unjust social system, or a society in which it is taken for granted that orphaned boys will sleep in boxes on the streets. To him (and, one presumes, to Alger), everything is determined by the efforts and the character of the individual. One of the contradictions in Alger's novels is that luck plays as large a part as the efforts of the boys. Gatsby actually begins by striving for advancement in the Alger method, with his daily schedule and with the intention to work his way through college as a janitor. However, he stayed at college only for two weeks, before abandoning the approved Alger route to success, and taking the one offered by Dan Cody. The Alger method would make Gatsby into a clerk, and keep him there, as it has Nick. Fitzgerald referred to this idea in 1930, when he angrily rejected some advice sent to him by his mother with the words: 'These would be good rules for a man who wanted to be a chief clerk at 50' (Fitzgerald, 1963, p. 496).

Fitzgerald satirizes the Alger ideals partly through Carraway who, again in contrast to Gatsby, is the model Alger boy. He comes to the East believing in the power of books, honesty, straightforwardness and regular study. Ironically, he turns down the lucky chance which would make him rich; and he turns it down because it conflicts with the ethical norms of an Alger boy. Fitzgerald's approach to the American dream as represented by Alger is that it promises advancement through hard work, but disguises the fact that advancement and upward mobility are impossible for most. It encouraged Americans to work hard, yet by so doing, helped to perpetuate a fairly rigid class system. This dichotomy between American beliefs and actuality persists today; a 1981 poll showed that 69 per cent of Americans believed that 'it is possible nowadays for someone in this country to start out poor and become rich by working hard' (Robertson, 1987, p. 274). In spite of this, the class mobility rates for the United States differ little from those for the United Kingdom. In the USA, as in the UK, most people remain in the same class as their parents.

The use Fitzgerald makes of the Wilsons brings together these concerns. The Wilsons represent the other side of the American dream, those who have worked hard in the belief that it will bring prosperity. On one level they represent failure, but their associations with the other characters suggest that in some way all the characters fail. The Wilsons are by no means rounded characters, though they are good examples of Fitzgerald's skill at sketching characters, at allowing one phrase or incident to stand for the whole character. The episode of Tom and Myrtle buying the dog is a good example (pp. 33–4); the scene establishes Myrtle's pretensions to gentility, and the 'crudeness' of Tom (Way, 1980, p. 111). One of the small proof changes Fitzgerald made had a similar effect. Originally, when Myrtle complained of the price charged by her chiropodist, she said, 'you'd of thought she had my appendix out'. In the proof, Fitzgerald altered 'appendix' to 'appendicitis' and thereby increased our sense of her pretensions (Eble, 1977, p. 93; *The Great Gatsby*, p. 37).

For all the satire of Myrtle, however, she is presented as an almost tragic figure. Fitzgerald repeatedly emphasizes her vitality, her blood, which are exceptional in both the valley of ashes and the novel's environment. She is someone prepared — desperately, perhaps — to enjoy life. But her earthiness turns farcical because of her pretensions, fed by gossip magazines and fiction. They feed her ideals of success, and in following them she becomes ridiculous. Wilson too seems ridiculous when he evokes the great dream of the opportunity of the West (p. 129). The illusions of potential success have resulted in their frustration and 'hollowness'.

The Wilsons are linked to the other characters in ways reminiscent of Fitzgerald's 'May Day'. Myrtle's physicality contrasts significantly both with Gatsby's idealized love, and with Daisy, who is characterized by her voice. The detail of Myrtle's breast 'swinging loose' (a detail which Fitzgerald considered essential [Fitzgerald, 1963, p. 175]), also sets up a contrast with the 'fresh green breast of the new world' that Carraway evokes at the close of the novel. Myrtle's 'thick dark blood' is mingled with the 'dust' (p. 144), and Carraway condemns everyone except Gatsby as 'foul dust' (p. 8). The relation between Myrtle, Tom and Wilson is curiously mirrored by that between Daisy, Gatsby and Tom; in this respect, it is not surprising that Myrtle's husband should kill Gatsby (having been sent to him by Tom).

If the corollary of success is represented by the Wilsons, by failure and frustration, then the symbol of failure is the hoarding advertising the practice of Dr Eckleburg. I indicated above that the suggestiveness of the symbol was the source of its power, but there are many sound reasons for considering that the eyes represent failure. It is implied that Eckleburg's practice has failed (p. 29), and they are set above Wilson's failing garage. But, more than that, they brood over the whole landscape, gigantic reminders of the failure that is always possible even for the temporarily successful. They indicate financial failure, but also the other failures of the novel; the moral, emotional and imaginative failures which Fitzgerald ultimately saw as the other side to the American dream of success.

The Great Gatsby and History

In 1940 Fitzgerald looked back on the time in which he wrote *The Great Gatsby* and said that he had also been reading the works of Oswald Spengler: 'I don't think I ever quite recovered from him. He and Marx are the only modern philosophers that still manage to make sense in this horrible mess' (Fitzgerald, 1963, pp. 289–90). Fitzgerald is referring specifically to Spengler's influential *The Decline of the West* (1918–1922). Some critics have pointed out that Fitzgerald's memory must have been confused, since a translation of the book was unavailable in America until 1926. However, Fitzgerald was usually well in touch with intellectual trends, and there is no reason to assume that he was not familiar with the general ideas of Spengler during the early 1920s; in fact, a summary of Spengler's thought was published in *The Dial* in 1924.

By comparing different cultures, Spengler came to the conclusion that civilizations have a defined life span, which reflects the biological cycle of youth, adolescence, maturity and senescence or decline. The maturity of a civilization is evident in its production and appreciation of art and music, and in the presence of a responsible aristocracy in a harmonious society. Decline is signalled by violence, social unrest, vulgarity and a decadent aristocracy. On the basis of comparative studies of cultures, he argued that Western civilization was entering its decline. Although Spengler is discredited now as a historian and a philosopher, the cyclical theory of history was tremendously influential at the time. It was by no means a new idea, but his work gave fresh impetus to it. The theory appealed especially to modernist writers, and modernism's major figures, W.B. Yeats, T.S. Eliot, Ezra Pound and James Joyce all referred to it in some way. The theory appealed to many because it helped explain an overwhelming sense of alienation and hopelessness felt after the war. *The Great Gatsby* belongs firmly in these contexts of modernism and the concerns of Spengler are taken over by Fitzgerald.

In many respects, *The Great Gatsby* is about the decline of America, the passing of its empire. The violence that seems ever present in the novel, from the breaking of Myrtle's nose to the ends of the people on Nick's list, embodies the culture's passage into a time of chaos and brutality. Even Tom Buchanan has an apocalyptic sense of the future, though, ironically, he also represents the decline into vulgarity and brutality. The Buchanans represent Spengler's corrupted aristocracy, who have power and prestige without any corresponding sense of responsibility to others. Gatsby himself is not exempt from the decline of the West; the fact that his dream is expressed materially in riches and in Daisy means that he has vulgarized a Romantic sense of beauty. Furthermore, he is Trimalchio, the parvenu who for Petronius represented the decline of the Roman Empire.

Even the seasonal changes in the novel echo Spengler's cycle. Spring is associated with the birth of civilization, with its founders and pioneers; its fullest maturity was symbolized by summer, and its decline by autumn and winter. It is thus striking that Nick moves to West Egg in late spring and leaves just before winter. Ironically, Nick echoes the birth of the American civilization. Having moved to the East, he is at first lonely, until someone 'more recently arrived' on West Egg asks him for directions. Having given them, Nick writes, 'I was lonely no longer. I was a guide, a pathfinder, an original settler' (p. 10). In this ironic way, the history of American settlement has, in the myth of *The Great Gatsby*, been stripped of its heroism and grandeur, and made both ironic and comical. The change from high summer to autumn in *The Great Gatsby* reflects the 'decline of the West'. And, of course, knowledge of Spengler adds point to Nick's otherwise perverse comment that all the major characters are 'Westerners'. They are Westerners in that they are inextricably involved in a culture which is breaking down. The repeated emphasis on time and the clock indicates not only the defeat of Gatsby's dream, but that time is running out for the civilization which is irreversibly in decline.

Those critics who have believed that *The Great Gatsby* is a kind of myth have usually cited the closing paragraphs as the strongest possible evidence for it. I would argue that the paragraphs do propose a myth, but it is the myth of decline. A close reading of the language of the final paragraphs reveals mainly the cynicism and pessimism that have run throughout the novel.

Fitzgerald prefaces, as it were, the closing paragraphs, by returning to an emphasis on Nick's perspective. Just as the novel's opening paragraphs establish his supposed authority, the closing ones remind us of Nick's point of view. He avoids the taxi driver's story of the accident and murder, and, tellingly, he erases the chalked obscenity which is visible 'clearly in the moonlight'. Nick is careful to inform us that his trunk is packed and his car sold 'to the grocer'; as though he can indulge in meditation about Gatsby only when these duties are completed. We recall that only in the preceding few pages, Nick has been seen obeying his social conscience by shaking hands with Jordan and Tom 'to leave things in order' (p. 184). Fitzgerald is prefacing the supposedly 'mythic' conclusion by reminding us of the characteristics of Nick that made Gatsby seem attractive. Nick is associated here with the grocer to whom his car has been sold. He has by now taken on the role of preserving the innocence of Gatsby; significantly, by ignoring and attempting to obliterate the perspectives of others on the event. It is as though he has a personal need to believe in Gatsby's innocence, and to preserve it. It is worth mentioning that this gesture of erasing the public obscenity is repeated by Holden Caulfield in J.D. Salinger's novel *The Catcher in the Rye* (1951). Holden wants to preserve the innocence of childhood and protect it against the corruption represented by the obscenity. Nick has by now become the protector of Gatsby's innocence. Fitzgerald is, then, carefully reminding us of Carraway's equivocal perspective, a perspective at once cynical and trusting of Gatsby.

When Carraway begins to tell us of the Dutch sailor approaching the 'fresh green breast of the new world' we can see the effects Fitzgerald achieved by shifting this paragraph from the first chapter to the end of the novel. By now, the reader cannot take the language at face value, because the words carry the connotations that Fitzgerald has created for them in the process of the novel. In particular, we are reminded of the detail of Myrtle's torn breast, and with 'green' Fitzgerald is reminding us of the green light on the Buchanan dock. This is no simple contrast between past and present; the idealism of the past contrasting with the lost ideals of the present. On the face of it, this may seem to be the case. Gatsby cannot match the sailors' capacity to wonder at the green breast of the new continent; he only has a green light before him, not a continent to be explored. But the symbols work in a much more complex way than such a simple contrast. The wonder of the sailors seems a reference to

Keats's poem 'On First Looking Into Chapman's Homer' which ends by referring (mistakenly) to the wonder of Cortez at being the first European to see the Pacific. But Fitzgerald's reference is ironic. The sailors have not come to admire the new continent disinterestedly; they are invaders who have come to exploit its settled people and seize its resources. Only a naïve attitude to history could result in an alternative belief. In any case, Fitzgerald's mention of the sailors is not an idle reference. The attentive reader recalls the novel's other sailor, Dan Cody. Again, the effect is not that of contrast, but of similarity. Cody's violence is not simply contrasted with the sailors' capacity for wonder; they are compatible. The sailors have come to ravage the 'breast' of the country as certainly as Cody will help destroy its supposed innocence. The closing paragraphs are not, then, setting up a simple contrast between past and present: they are suggesting that the past which myth has idealized was itself corrupt. America itself was founded not in disinterested idealism but in the desire for resource and materials.

Even the comparison between the green breast of the continent and the green light on Daisy's dock is not a positive one. After all, the novel has just shown how Gatsby's belief led to disillusionment and to his death. In some ways, he was betrayed by his capacity for belief. In any case, Fitzgerald's collocation of 'green' with 'breast' brings together both Daisy and Myrtle. The non-physical idealism of Gatsby towards Daisy is bound up here with Tom's straightforwardly physical relation to Myrtle. Both are present in the wonder of the sailors, but their capacity to wonder lasts only for a moment.

Interestingly, relatively few critics have commented upon the closing line of the novel, 'So we beat on, boats against the current, borne back ceaselessly into the past' (p. 188). But several of its features are striking. Fitzgerald shifts from the individual Gatsby to the generic 'us'; a shift similar to that made by T.S. Eliot from 'I' to 'We' at the end of 'The Love Song of J. Alfred Prufrock'. But the preceding paragraph has made it clear that Gatsby's dream is not 'our' dream. Gatsby believes in the future, but the 'us' of the final line is borne back always into the past; that is, because the present proves unresponsive to our dreams, we continually idealize the past. The sailors' wonder was momentary; afterwards, it became a memory that succeeding

generations have turned into a myth. The final paragraphs are
not so much about myth as about the capacity to make myths
and fictions, to believe in them even when the relation they have
to reality is minimal. Nick is 'brooding' over these ideas in the
way that the eyes of Eckleburg brood over the valley of ashes.
The end of the novel does not make Gatsby heroic. It maintains
the dichotomy that has prevailed during Nick's narrative, and it
extends his pessimism about the future into history. These final
paragraphs are cynical and pessimistic. In them Fitzgerald's lack
of faith in the future is matched by his recognition of the human
tendency to mythologize and idealize the past.

References

Adams, J. T., *The Epic of America* (London, 1932).

Anderson, Richard, 'Gatsby's Long Shadow', in Bruccoli (1985) pp. 15–40.

Barbour, Brian, '*The Great Gatsby* and the American Past', *The Southern Review*, IX (1973), 288–99.

Barrett, William, 'Fitzgerald and America', *Partisan Review*, XVIII (1951), 345–53.

Bewley, Marius, 'Scott Fitzgerald's Criticism of America', *The Sewanee Review*, LXII (1954), 223–46; repr. in Lockridge (1968), pp. 37–53.

Bicknell, John W., 'The Waste Land of F. Scott Fitzgerald', *Virginia Quarterly Review*, XXX (1954), 556–72.

Bruccoli, Matthew (ed.), *New Essays on 'The Great Gatsby'* (Cambridge, 1985).

Bruccoli, Matthew, 'Introduction ' to Bruccoli (1985), pp. 1–14.

Bryer, Jackson R. (ed.), *The Short Stories of F. Scott Fitzgerald: New Approaches in Criticism* (Madison, Wisconsin, 1982).

Callahan, John F., *The Illusions of A Nation: Myth and History in the Novels of F. Scott Fitzgerald* (Urbana, Illinois, 1972).

Carlisle, E. Fred, 'The Triple Vision of Nick Carraway', *Modern Fiction Studies*, XI (1965–66), 351–60.

Chase, Richard, '*The Great Gatsby*', in *The Modern Novel and Its Tradition* (New York, 1957), pp. 162–7; repr. in Hoffman (1962), pp. 297–302.

Conrad, Joseph, *The Nigger of the Narcissus* (New York, 1967 [1897]).

Doyno, Victor, 'Patterns in *The Great Gatsby*', *Modern Fiction Studies*, XII (1966), 415–26.

Dyson, A. E., 'The Great Gatsby: Thirty-Six Years After', Modern Fiction Studies, VII (1961), 37–48.

Eble, Kenneth, F. Scott Fitzgerald (Boston, 1964; rev. edn, 1977).

Fitzgerald, F. Scott, This Side of Paradise (New York: Scribners, 1920; Harmondsworth, 1971).

Fitzgerald, F. Scott, 'An Introduction to The Great Gatsby' (New York, 1934), pp. vii–xi; repr. in Lockridge (1968), pp. 108–10.

Fitzgerald, F. Scott, The Crack-Up, ed. Edmund Wilson (New York, 1956).

Fitzgerald, F. Scott, The Letters of F. Scott Fitzgerald, ed. Andrew Turnbull (London, 1963).

Fitzgerald, F. Scott, The Crack-Up with Other Pieces and Stories (Harmondsworth, 1974).

Fitzgerald, F. Scott, The Collected Short Stories of F. Scott Fitzgerald (Harmondsworth, 1987).

Forster, E. M., Aspects of the Novel (Harmondsworth, 1976 [1927]), pp. 73–84.

Fussell, Edwin, 'Fitzgerald's Brave New World', English Literary History, XIX (1952), 291–306; rev. version repr. in Hoffman (1962), pp. 244–62.

Garrett, George, 'Fire and Freshness: A Matter of Style in The Great Gatsby', in Bruccoli (1985), pp. 101–16.

Giles, Barbara, 'The Dream of F. Scott Fitzgerald', Mainstream, X (March 1957), 1–12.

Hanzo, Thomas, 'The Theme and Narrator of The Great Gatsby', Modern Fiction Studies, II (1957), 183–90; repr. in Lockridge (1968), pp. 61–9.

Harvey, W. J., 'Theme and Texture in The Great Gatsby', English Studies, XXXVIII (1957), 12–20; repr. in Lockridge (1968), pp. 90–100.

Hemingway, Ernest, The Snows of Kilimanjaro and Other Stories (New York, 1961).

Hoffman, Frederick J. (ed.), The Great Gatsby: A Study (New York, 1962).

Hoffman, Frederick J., 'Introduction' to Hoffman (1962), pp. 1–18.

Isaacs, Neil D., ' "Winter Dreams" and Summer Sports', in Bryer (1982), pp. 199–207.

Korenman, Joan S., ' "Only her Hairdresser . . . ": Another Look at Daisy Buchanan', *American Literature*, XLVI (1975), 547–8.

Le Vot, André, *F. Scott Fitzgerald: A Biography* (London, 1984 [translated by William Byron]), pp. 137–67.

Lehan, Richard D., *F. Scott Fitzgerald and the Craft of Fiction* (Carbondale, Illinois, 1966).

Lewis, Roger, 'Money, Love and Aspiration in *The Great Gatsby*', in Bruccoli (1985), pp. 41–57.

Lisca, Peter, 'Nick Carraway and the Imagery of Disorder', *Twentieth Century Literature*, XIII (1967), 18–28.

Lockridge, Ernest (ed.), *Twentieth Century Interpretations of 'The Great Gatsby'* (Englewood Cliffs, NJ, 1968).

Lockridge, Ernest, 'Introduction' to Lockridge (1968), pp. 1–18.

Long, Robert E., '*The Great Gatsby* and the Tradition of Joseph Conrad', *Texas Studies in Literature and Language*, VIII (1966), 257–76, 407–22.

Lundberg, Ferdinand, *The Rich and the Super-Rich* (New York, 1968).

Malin, Irving, ' "Absolution": Absolving Lies', in Bryer (1982), pp. 209–16.

Miller, James E., *F Scott Fitzgerald: His Art and His Technique* (New York, 1964; rev. edn, 1967).

Mizener, Arthur, *The Far Side of Paradise* (Boston, 1951).

Mizener, Arthur, *Scott Fitzgerald* (London, 1972).

Ornstein, Robert, 'Scott Fitzgerald's Fable of East and West', *College English*, XVIII (1957), 139–43; repr. in Lockridge (1968), pp. 54–60.

Parr, Susan Resneck, 'The Idea of Order at West Egg', in Bruccoli (1985), pp. 59–78.

Perkins, Maxwell, 'Letter to Scott Fitzgerald', 1925, repr. in Lockridge (1968), pp. 101–3.

Perosa, Sergio, *The Art of F. Scott Fitzgerald* (Ann Arbor, Michigan, 1965 [translated by the author and Charles Matz]).

Piper, Henry Dan, *F. Scott Fitzgerald: A Candid Portrait* (New York, 1962) part repr. in Hoffman (1962), pp. 321–34.

Robertson, Ian, *Sociology* (New York, 1987).

Salinger, J. D., *The Catcher in the Rye* (Boston, 1951).

Samuels, Charles Thomas, 'The Greatness of *Gatsby*', *Massachusetts Review*, VII (1966), 783–94.

Scrimgeour, Gary J., 'Against *The Great Gatsby*', *Criticism*, VIII (1966), 75–86; repr. in Lockridge (1968), pp. 70–81.

Sklar, Robert, *F. Scott Fitzgerald: The Last Laocoön* (London, 1967).

Stallman, R. W., 'Gatsby and the Hole in Time', in *The Houses that James Built* (East Lansing, Michigan, 1961), pp. 131–50.

Trilling, Lionel, *The Liberal Imagination* (London, 1950), pp. 250–4; repr. in Lockridge (1968), pp. 110–13.

Troy, William, 'The Authority of Failure', *Accent*, VI (1945), 56–60; repr. in Hoffman (1962), pp. 224–31.

Tuttleton, James, W. 'Seeing Slightly Red: Fitzgerald's "May Day"', in Bryer (1982), pp. 181–97.

Vanderbilt, Kermit, 'James, Fitzgerald and the American Self-Image', *Massachusetts Review*, VI (Winter–Spring, 1965), 289–304.

Watt, Ian, *The Rise of the Novel* (London, 1957).

Way, Brian, *F. Scott Fitzgerald and the Art of Social Fiction* (London, 1980).

Westbrook, J. S., 'Nature and Optics in *The Great Gatsby*', *American Literature*, XXXII (1960), 78–84.

Wharton, Edith, 'Letter to F. Scott Fitzgerald', 1925, repr. in Lockridge (1968), pp. 106–7.

Wilson, Edmund, 'F. Scott Fitzgerald', *Bookman* (March, 1922), 27–35; repr. in Hoffman (1962), pp. 21–8.

Wimsatt, W. K. and Beardsley, Monroe, 'The Intentional Fallacy' and 'The Affective Fallacy', in Wimsatt, *The Verbal Icon* (Lexington, Kentucky, 1954).

Wolfe, Peter, 'Faces in a Dream: Innocence Perpetuated in "The Rich Boy"', in Bryer (1982), pp. 241–9.

Further Reading

Several of the collections of criticism referred to in the text are excellent further reading which I would highly recommend. The selection edited by Frederick Hoffman (1962), is especially good, though perhaps less readily available than Ernest Lockridge's selection for the *Twentieth Century Views* series (1968). *New Essays on 'The Great Gatsby'*, edited by Matthew Bruccoli, is an often stimulating collection of more recent essays (1985). Among the general books on F. Scott Fitzgerald, I would especially recommend those by Kenneth Eble (1977), Brian Way (1980), John F. Callahan (1972), Richard Lehan (1966) and James E. Miller (1967).

As I noted above, the interest in Fitzgerald's life has stimulated several biographies. Arthur Mizener's critical biography (1951) is still very readable, and that by André Le Vot (1984) is similarly accessible. As well as critical reading, however, I would strongly recommend the reading of Fitzgerald's other novels and his short stories. They are not only of great interest in themselves, and enjoyable to read, but they will add to one's appreciation of the achievement represented by *The Great Gatsby*.

Index